REVELATIONS

REVELATIONS

ON THE AIR

a paranoid novel
of suspense by
BARRY N.
MALZBERG

with an
introduction by
D. HARLAN
WILSON

AØP
ANTI-OEDIPUS PRESS

Revelations
Copyright © 1972 by Barry N. Malzberg
ISBN: 978-0-99-915354-3
Library of Congress Control Number: 2020934879

First published in the United States by Warner Paperback

First Anti-Oedipal Paperback Edition: March 2020

www.rawdogscreaming.com

Introduction © 2020 by D. Harlan Wilson
Afterword © 1976 by Barry N. Malzberg
Afterword to an Afterword © 2019 by Barry N. Malzberg

Cover Design by Matthew Revert
www.matthewrevert.com

Interior Layout by D. Harlan Wilson
www.dharlanwilson.com

Anti-Oedipus Press
Grand Rapids, MI

www.anti-oedipuspress.com

PRAISE FOR BARRY N. MALZBERG

"There are possibly a dozen genius writers in the genre of the imaginative, and Barry Malzberg is at least eight of them."

—Harlan Ellison

"Malzberg makes persuasively clear that the best of science fiction should be valued as literature and nothing else."

—*The Washington Post*

"One of the finest practitioners of science fiction."

—Harry Harrison

"Barry N. Malzberg's writing is unparalleled in its intensity and in its apocalyptic sensibility. His detractors consider him bleakly monotonous and despairing, but he is a master of black humor, and is one of the few writers to have used science fiction's vocabulary of ideas extensively as apparatus in psychological landscapes, dramatizing relationships between the human mind and its social environment in an SF theater of the absurd."

—*The Encyclopedia of Science Fiction*

"The writer who attempts to use the SF mythos as Malzberg has is bedevilled by the inappropriateness of the 'rules' pertaining to the production and consumption of mass-produced fiction."

—Brian Stableford

"Malzberg is a true hero."

—*The Magazine of Fantasy & Science Fiction*

"There is no one, with the possible exception of Philip K. Dick, whose works, each one of them, are so unpredictable or so outrageous and outraged."

—Theodore Sturgeon

"Barry Malzberg is one of science fiction's most literate and erudite writers."

—*New York Times Book Review*

BOOKS BY BARRY N. MALZBERG

NOVELS

FICTION COLLECTIONS

Out from Ganymede
The Many Worlds of Barry Malzberg
Down Here in the Dream Quarter
The Best of Barry Malzberg
Malzberg at Large
The Man Who Loved the Midnight Lady
The Passage of the Light
In the Stone House
On Account of Darkness and Other SF Stories
The Very Best of Barry N. Malzberg

NONFICTION

Breakfast in the Ruins
The Engines of the Night
The Business of Science Fiction

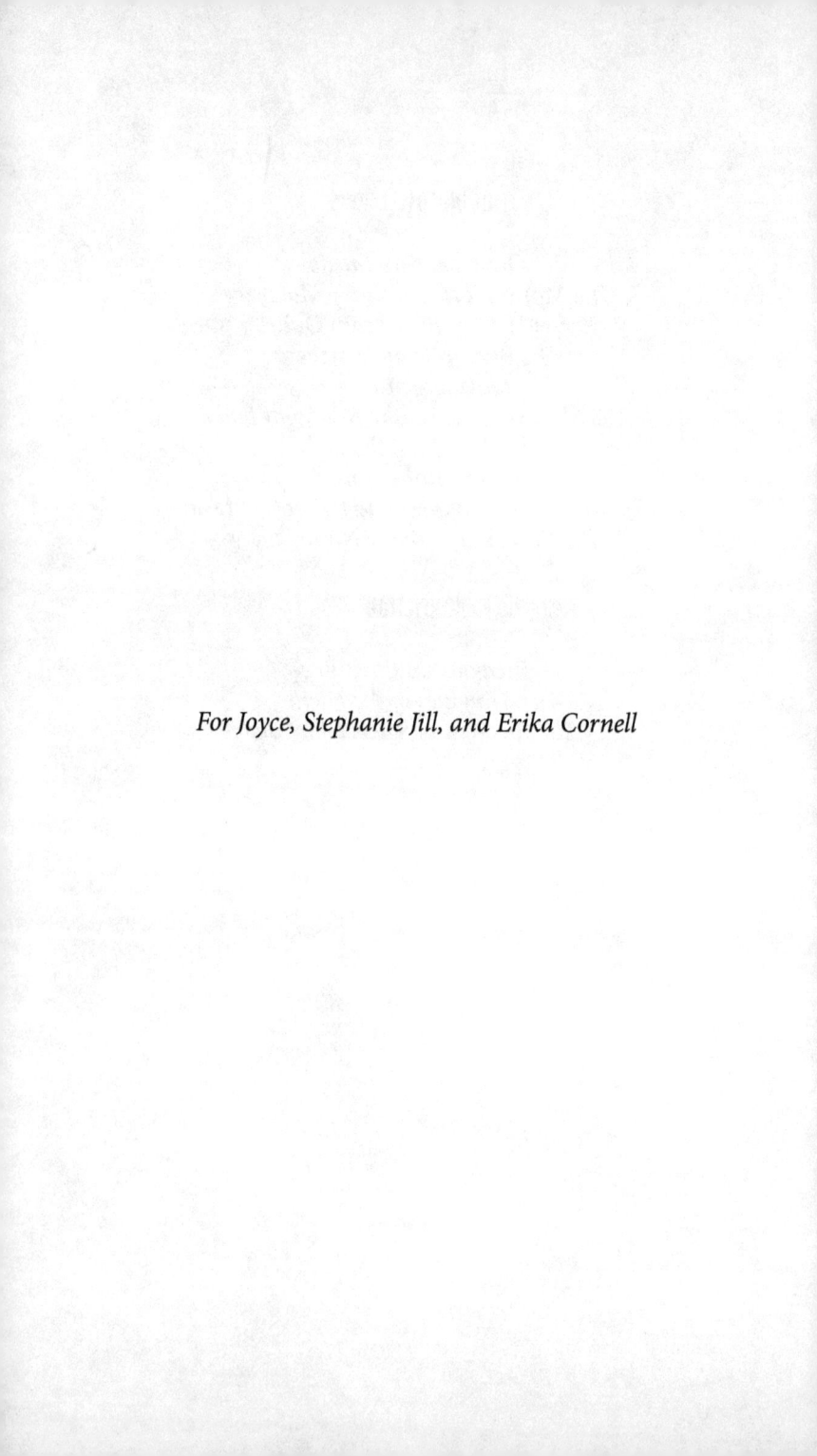

For Joyce, Stephanie Jill, and Erika Cornell

Drowning beneath ice, I see
Possibility; just
Breathing would keep me:
I'd melt it, have my breath.

I lack
That animal eye that sees
Everything, blinks,
And then opens the camera in sunlight.

Lovers
Skate out my face. Effortless
That scribbling in the close cold; whole
Bahamas of the blood beneath their coats.

—Trim Bissell: *Inside* (1968)

INTRODUCTION
MALZBERG AND I: THE GRAVITY OF SCIENCE FICTION

D. Harlan Wilson

Nobody can finesse a semicolon like Barry N. Malzberg . . .

We barely remember what a semicolon is anymore. I have been a college professor for twenty years, and my students don't know what to do with this weird article of punctuation. All they know is that it forms the eyes of a primitive emoji when it's juxtaposed with a parenthesis. Like so:

;)

Removed from the parenthesis, all hell breaks loose. And hell is best ignored. This cryptic symbol located beneath the colon on computer keyboards—if we recognize it at all, we abjure it.

At some point in our schooling, we learn (and immediately forget) that semicolons function like periods; the only difference is that they link together two independent, inter-related clauses, as in this very sentence. Semicolons are also used to divide lists of items that contain commas in their syntax: in this instance, they function like commas. They are the shapeshifters of the punctuation world, evolved and fluid, multi-purpose dogpoets in a maelstrom of singularities. But semicolons are not lawless. Like all punctuation marks, they abide by fixed rules of conduct.

Throughout his career, Malzberg unfixed these rules and scattered them across the canvas of his milieu with the same wild abandon as he dismantled the rules of the science fiction genre.

The semicolon can mean or do anything in a Malzberg novel. He makes the semicolon his own, deploying it for a dramatic pause, a frenetic cue, an existential talisman, a means of syntactic inscription that empowers an innovates the identity of a sentence. Likewise did he make SF his own. The genre didn't care. It cares even less today, especially in light of how the anvil of reality has usurped so many of its machinations, turning what was once the so-called "genre of ideas" into the junk of naught.

Science fiction is a twentieth-century artifact.

As a genre of ideas, two movements distinguish SF: the New Wave of the 1960s and cyberpunk of the 1980s. Everything else is noise, spin, and riff—even cyberpunk, to some degree, which extrapolated the avant-garde efforts of the New Wave. All this presumes the validity of a "movement." As Malzberg has noted, there are "no literary movements, merely a bunch of writers sometimes hanging out together and trying to do their work" ("Fifties" 55). These days, movements are almost invariably marketing ploys. That's fine; if nothing else, authors sell a few more books, and scholars have something to write about. In the case of the New Wave, however, the term was borrowed from French experimental film criticism, then applied to a bunch of writers by reviewers and critics, with the first usage belonging to P. Schuyler Miller in his book-review column "The Reference Library" in 1961 ("New").

Everything coalesced in the New Wave, a speakeasy that subverted the prohibitions of pulp and Golden Age SF. It was the apex of SF as a source of genuine innovation, and cyberpunk was a stylish coda. In his famous preface to *Mirrorshades: A Cyberpunk Anthology*, Bruce Sterling foregrounds the influence of New Wave authors:

> The cyberpunks as a group are steeped in the lore and tradition of the SF field. Their precursors are legion. Individual cyberpunk writers differ in their literary debts; but some older writers, ancestral cyberpunks perhaps, show a clear and striking influence. From the New Wave: the streetwise edginess of Harlan Ellison. The visionary shimmer of Samuel Delany. The free-wheeling zaniness of Norman Spinrad and the rock esthetic of Michael Moorcock; the intellectual daring of Brian Aldiss; and, always, J.G. Ballard. (x)

No mention of Malzberg. No Philip K. Dick either, although Sterling invokes Malzberg's closest American counterpart later in the preface.

Spurred by Moorcock's editorship of *New Worlds*, the New Wave took flight in the United Kingdom. It bled into American culture most pointedly in the *Dangerous Visions* anthologies edited by Harlan Ellison. The second volume, *Again, Dangerous Visions*, featured Malzberg's "Still-Life," a story published under the pseudonym K.M. O'Donnell that Ellison called "a new kind of fiction . . . I wish I could invent a term like 'neorealistic' or 'fabulated' . . . but frankly I cannot even devise a category" (281). Herein lies one of

Malzberg/O'Donnell's great powers: the deflection of category (i.e., the author as a genre in himself), an angle of repose and inimitability that few authors enjoy or have the sand to actually beget. Elsewhere, Ellison had this to say: "There are possibly a dozen genius writers in the genre of the imaginative, and Barry Malzberg is at least eight of them. He makes what the rest of us do look like felonies!"

Despite this much-deserved praise, Malzberg proved to be too much of a rogue even for the New Wave. After a burst of productivity in the genre that included over 20 books and 150 stories ("Rage"), he had all but eaten the sunset by the time Sterling, William Gibson, Pat Cadigan, et al. had made their mark. The engines of the night rusted away. All that remained was breakfast in the ruins . . .

Wary of the raw potential of SF, "a dangerous literature represent[ing] the beast born in the era of enlightenment to snarl at the heart of all intellectual and technological advance," but consistently frustrated by the "hostility of the culture, the ineptitude of many of its practitioners, the loathing of most of its editors, the corruption of most of its readers," Malzberg cultivated a literature that was distinctly, unapologetically, unwaveringly *his own*, recognizing that the problem with the genre was (and remains) its relative malleability and consequent indefinability ("Number" 17). "It is an ambivalent genre and I have been, perhaps, its most ambivalent writer," he admitted in 1979. "The career and Collected Works, the life itself, have been a mausoleum to schism. The field is one thing and yet it may be the other. I am one thing and yet the other. I, the field, may be both but somehow I doubt it. One cannot embrace multitudes; one can barely (and only then if life is lived well) embrace oneself. There is simply no conclusion" ("Science" 86). Self-aware and self-effacing, as the best writers are, Malzberg had a clear idea about where SF should go if it wanted to make good on its prerogative to be the supreme literature of the imagination, but there were too many short-sighted, short-shrifting, shit-eating Little Men in the way. And the Little Men got their way.

In "Something Is Broken in Our Science Fiction," Lee Konstantinou catalogs the long list of punk SF subgenres that have materialized in the wake of cyberpunk, such as "steampunk, biopunk, nanopunk, stonepunk, clockpunk, rococopunk, raypunk, nowpunk, atompunk, mannerpunk, salvagepunk, Trumppunk, solarpunk, and sharkpunk." Like a successful TV series whose producers will do anything to milk it for as many seasons as possible, this "proliferation of SF punks is what you'd expect from the overproduction of popular culture," but all "postcyberpunk" formations—postmodernism, poststructuralism, postindustrialism, or postwhatever—are markers of absurdism and ultimately death: the prefix "post" simply means that a group of would-be ideologists (usually intellectuals, authors, and artists trying to make a name for themselves and their work) don't know what to do, where to go, or who they are, because there's *nothing* beyond *post*.

If they were intended as sheer satire and burlesque, punk and post subgenres might be worth some attention. Unfortunately, most of the authors and editors involved with these formations (and with SF on the whole) are dead serious. It is a deficiency, this seriousness, this *gravity* that pulls them down, gluing them firmly in place, this *affect* that symptomatizes their anxieties and insecurities about their imaginative output. They are so grave about SF, they fail to see that the genre is just that: in the grave, rotting, where they put it.

Konstantinou suggests that contemporary SF lacks the glint of newness visible in the novels and stories of numerous authors associated with cyberpunk (and, by extension, the New Wave):

> It's easy to see why some writers, editors, and critics have failed to think very far beyond the horizon cyberpunk helped define. If the best you can do is worm your way through gleaming arcologies you played little part in building—if your answer to dystopia is to develop some new anti-authoritarian style, attitude, or ethos—you might as well give up the game, don your mirrorshades, and admit you're still doing cyberpunk (close to four decades later). But if this is your choice, if you're writing science fiction that decides on its attitude toward the future in advance of doing the work of imagining that future, you're not heeding the most ambitious calling of the genre. You've substituted the hunt for a cool new market niche for the work of telling compelling stories that help us think rigorously about how we might make a better world, or at the very least better understand where our world might be heading.

Konstantinou presumes that good SF must be futuristic, which, of course, isn't always true. He also doesn't account for the degree to which modern technology has leveled the playing field so that Team Reality (or Team Nonfiction) has become indistinct from Team Science Fiction. This seems to have escaped some readers and writers. Overall, it has little to do with the innovative abilities of the genre. In the year 10,000 A.D., if we're still around, SF will harbor the same potential that it does today. The problem is that almost nobody harvests that potential.

The problem, in other words, is the people who inhabit the desert of science fiction. I have come to know many

SF writers, readers, and editors over the years. To put it delicately, there is a fundamental disconnect among these people and the way in which they perceive the apple of their collective eye. Desire, as always, is a problem, too. What they *want* does not necessarily accord with what should *be* (or, if you like, what Malzberg and I *want to be*).

In a 1992 meditation, "On Decadence," Malzberg says that cyberpunk (a term he dislikes) is just another response to cultural forces (e.g., late capitalism, MTV, VCRs, home computers, the Cold War, etc.), but not without significant effects. "Cyberpunk," he writes,

> made narcissism a true and functional value and managed to link that narcissism to the continuing skein of the field, find antecedents in the bulkier computer and cyborg devices of the 40s and 50s . . . and drag the work toward a context which was found identifiable by a lot of people who were not otherwise writing science fiction. That is one form of irresolution masquerading as resolve; another would be the explosion of alternate histories, alternate worlds, alternate historical placements. (259)

What he doesn't mention—and what matters more to me, and what Malzberg himself was doing—is how cyberpunks amped up the literary project initiated by the New Wave via *the art of language*, further distancing the genre from the crummy writing that has plagued and dominated it since its inception. Language is as good a novum as any other science fictional artifice, be it tangible, intangible, or in this instance, rhetorical. In my view, it's the best novum. Technically it's the *only* novum: there is no writing without words, after all. And unlike 99% of his peers, the art of language—not just how it looks, but how it moves, how it flows, how it blusters and wallows and burns—is another one of Malzberg's terrific strengths.

I discovered Malzberg when I was working on my M.A. in Science Fiction Studies at the University of Liverpool, a program that is, sadly, now defunct (academia seems to be mirroring the SF genre's decay). While it wasn't part of my coursework, a fellow graduate student recommended *Beyond Apollo* to me, and I was hooked. In retrospect, it was the palpable sense of the absurd that resonated with me. Malzberg wasn't just a terrific writer, he was funny, too. Published in 1972, *Beyond Apollo* features a recurrent Malzbergian trickster: the mad astronaut. The novel satirizes the bureaucratic machinery of NASA's Apollo program with a Kafkaesque flair unmatched by any other SF author (even Philip K. Dick, maybe the most important postwar SF author, yet not a wordsmith of the same caliber). The subject matter is serious business, but Malzberg wears it like a cape, plunging into weird, irreal, and erotic interzones that his more earnest, unsmiling peers wouldn't dare touch. Other classic SF novels published in the early 1970s include Larry Niven's *Ringworld* (1970), Philip José Farmer's *To Your Scattered Bodies Go* (1971), Arthur C. Clarke's *Rendezvous with Rama* (1973), Joe Haldeman's *The Forever War* (1974), Ursula K. Le Guin's *The Dispossessed* (1974), and J.G. Ballard's *High-Rise* (1975)—all significant books, but none of them came close to what Malzberg did in *Beyond Apollo*. I can't speak for Malzberg's authorial intent or frame of mind. It's clear, however, that he was taking risks.

Notwithstanding *Beyond Apollo*'s biting tone, graphic sexuality, unreliable narrator, aggressive ambiguity, icy nihilism, and negative representation of the space program, the novel won the first annual John W. Campbell Award. I like to think that it was too distinctive, absorbing, and well-written to ignore or turn away, but I suspect there were political motives. According to Irish SF novelist Bob Shaw, "Malzberg's *Beyond Apollo* is, to me, the epitome of everything that has gone wrong with SF in the last ten years or so" (qtd. in Pringle 36). In fact, it was one of the only things to have gone right.

I wrote my M.A. thesis on decidedly non-Malzbergian material: Dan Simmons' Hyperion Cantos. At the time, I was interested in Simmons' appropriation of Romanticism, especially Keats. I continued to read Malzberg on the sly, moving from *Beyond Apollo* to *Galaxies* (1975), *The Falling Astronauts* (1971), *Herovit's World* (1973), *The Remaking of Sigmund Freud* (1985), and *Revelations* (1972), all of which had gone out of print. This was in the late 1990s; Amazon and eBay were still in diapers, and obscure books were hard to come by. Luckily, the University of Liverpool had one of the largest SF collections in the world. I could access primary and secondary texts that otherwise would have been out of reach to me. Books in the collection couldn't be checked out, and I specifically recall taking notes on *Galaxies* in the basement of the university library.

In subsequent years, I read and reread more Malzberg, including his SF as well as his crime fiction, erotica, and nonfiction. Whatever the format or genre, I found consistent inspiration for my own stories and novels. Above all, perhaps, I'm drawn to the metafictional techniques that galvanize and deepen his sizable body of work, particularly when those techniques take the form of critifiction levied against The Little Men Who Deserve It.

When I founded Anti-Oedipus Press in 2013, one of my primary objectives was to republish special editions of exceptional yet unconventional books that had been taken out of print. Malzberg was at the top of the list. As a result of his persistent nonconformity and avant-garde dash, his oeuvre has been widely underappreciated and ignored, and yet I have never met or talked to anybody about Malzberg who had read his writing and didn't love it. He might be the SF genre's greatest anomaly. At the very least, he amassed a cult following that still has teeth.

In 2014, Anti-Oedipus Press republished *Galaxies*. This was our third release. In 2015, we brought *Beyond Apollo* back into print, then *The Falling Astronauts* in 2017, and now *Revelations*, which was written between these two novels and shares common themes. Together they form a loose trilogy in which the protagonists face similar existential crises driven by bureaucratic toxicity and venomous media forces. *Revelations* in particular anticipates the media pathology that has come to roost in the form of reality television and social networks where people go to any length to turn themselves into celebrities. The gods of war now exist on Instagram, YouTube, Snapchat, and TikTok. They have no talent, no brains, no shame, and limitless power. Welcome to *Revelations*: I'm Marvin Martin, your antagonist and parasitic host . . .

Revelations satirizes talk shows popular in the 1960s and early 1970s, probably *The Tonight Show* more than anything, with Marvin Martin parodying Johnny Carson, but the novel also gestures toward paparazzi culture and mass-media warlords like TMZ. In this regime, anything goes, anything can be done, anybody can be violated and hung out to dry, sans taboo, sans decorum or accountability, all in the name of consumer-capitalism and the Terminal Image.

Reviewers have said that Malzberg's novels are too confusing, too nonlinear, too nebulous, too dense, too rude, too unscrupulous, and ultimately too "weird."

Science fiction doesn't know what weird is. None of the speculative genres know what it is. Even Weird and New Weird fiction doesn't have a clue. The problem is they *think* they do. Nearly all speculative fiction has always adhered to a transparent morality of staunch conservatism and crass, incessant, anti-innovative capitulation. Throughout history, the SF authors to whom this rule doesn't apply can be itemized very quickly.

Objectivity is a myth. Everything is subjective. I can only speak for myself here, and I can only view the world and make sense of it through these eyes, with these neurons, although I've read and studied and written about thousands of books, and in the narrative of my subjectivity, objectivity is a meek antagonist, a Little Man's sidekick at best. I recognize that most readers don't like what I like. For instance, I really enjoy short novels with stylized prose, flat characters, and mosaic plots that confuse me and thrive on nonsense, reifying Kurt Vonnegut's (dis)avowal that "in nonsense is strength" (10). In general, most readers of any genre enjoy the antithesis of everything I just mentioned when they read a book. They like longer novels with idiomatic prose, round characters, and straight-shooting plots that make sense and are easy to follow. And there's books aplenty for them to read that are written this way. Millions of them. But this isn't literature. It's a pastime, silage for the proles, something to do in airports and doctor's offices. Literature makes readers think, challenges their expectations and ideologies, probes the psyche and grapples with the Unknown, unlocks and exposes the mysteries and wonders and hilarities of the human condition, and it does these things through the medium of language that is carefully constructed, if not rhythmic and musical. Literature also preserves its roots, nostalgic for its own kind and a time when an author's m.o. wasn't solely to write books than can be easily adapted into movies.

In short, "good" writing that is truly "weird" is literature, which exhibits an inherent pursuit of innovation. In stride with his modernist precursors, New Wave contemporaries, and cyberpunk successors, Malzberg wrote literature.

Make it new.

In 1928, when Ezra Pound's famous slogan first appeared in his translation of *Da Xue*, he wasn't thinking about SF or what was called "scientific fiction." Two years earlier, Hugo Gernsback turned SF into a portmanteau word in the debut issue of *Amazing Stories*, christening it "scientifiction," but Pound and company were out of the loop and didn't realize that the potential for innovation dormant in SF was cut from the same elemental cloth that they were spinning for their own work. As I have discussed, it wasn't until the New Wave and cyberpunk that a meaningful collision of inventiveness would come to bear. Finally, SF seemed to be primed to blast off to the stars, but it's been mostly downhill since the 1980s. Gravity has had its ways with the genre.

Don't get me wrong. The modernists are vastly overrated. Joyce's *Ulysses* (1922) is a terrible book, despite being thoroughly science fictional and novum-centric—contrary to the scholarly mythos, it's tedious, affected, kind of stupid, poorly written, and nowhere near as clever as it thinks it is. Stein is even more boring and plodding: the ennui generated by *The Making of Americans* (1925) requires an anti-depressant prescription. Pound's writing is so pretentious and forced that I can hear his cravat flapping in the wind even as I plod through his Big Poems. Faulkner: dry as dust. Beckett: not funny enough. Hemingway: I still can't believe *The Old Man and Sea* (1952) won the Pulitzer—how did it even get published? Eliot: I like it when "Prufrock" ends and everybody drowns. Ellison: overrated. Fitzgerald: meh. Okay, Kafka and Woolf are great, but who cares? The point is, they were all writing literature, trying to *make it new* in their own unique ways. Such a collective effort not only doesn't exist anymore, the very idea of it is treated with scorn and trepidation. We disdain what we fear and don't understand, and the modernist project escapes almost everybody who lives in our science fictional reality, whether they read the Good, the Bad, the Ugly, or nothing.

Regarding twenty-first-century SF's cryo-generic state of rigor mortis, I'm not going to badmouth anybody by name. I'll take the heat for it, just as Malzberg did when Thomas M. Disch called him out for not fingering the riffraff in *Engines of the Night*, preferring to talk "in vast, gasping generalities about the swamp and pity of it all" ("Engines" 211). I will say that, with a few proverbial exceptions—most of whom aren't even considered SF writers, and they certainly don't write hard or genre SF—I condemn all contemporary practitioners as a whole. "They are silly, childish people" (434)—Alfred Bester's 1961 thesis in "A Diatribe Against Science Fiction" still holds true today. The only authors trying to making anything new in 2020 were among the few authors trying to make things new in the twentieth century. And for the most part, they've stopped trying. No worries. Netflix and Pornhub are infinitely more important than science fiction literature.

For you unborn Zarathustrians who prefer the screaming Twilight to the hollow Idols of image-culture, however, I invite you to start here, with *Revelations*, as fine an introduction as any into the House of Malzberg. Like all good anti-oedipal ventures, one may enter the House from any doorway, at any speed or angle of incidence, dressed in a tux or undressed altogether, happy and content or angry, deranged, and feral. What you will encounter is unrivaled feng shui that, as Gilles Deleuze and Félix Guattari explain in *A Thousand Plateaus* (1980), "imitates the world, as art imitates nature: by procedures specific to it that accomplish what nature cannot or can no longer do" (Deleuze 5).

P.S. By force of immersion, the narrator of the above introduction channels Malzberg; as such, he is unreliable and mostly fictional: hardly any of his assholery belongs to the "real" D. Harlan Wilson, and he lies like a dog (e.g., D. loves all of those modernist authors that I badmounth on pages xxii and xxiii). I tend to let the material I work with infect me, if only for metanarrational kicks. That said, I do really wish more writers would take risks and aspire for the New. What's the fun in doing what's been done? Qua Deleuze and Guattari in *L'Anti-Œdipe* (1972): "*Il n'y a que l'idée pour injecter le venin*" (372).

—**Betty Lomax**
Dreamfield, Ohio, 2022

BIBLIOGRAPHY

Bester, Alfred. "A Diatribe Against Science Fiction." 1961. *Redemolished*. ibooks. 2000.

Deleuze, Gilles and Félix Guattari. *A Thousand Plateaus*. 1980. Trans. Brian Massumi. Minnesota UP, 2000.

——. *L'Anti-Œdipe*. Les Éditions de Minuet, 1972.

Ellison, Harlan. Cover Blurb. *Herovit's World*. Random House, 1973.

——. "Introduction to 'Still-Life'." *Again, Dangerous Visions*. Doubleday, 1972. 280-81.

Konstantinou, Lee. "Something Is Broken in Our Science Fiction." *Slate.com*. Jan. 15, 2019. https://slate.com/technology/2019/01/hopepunk-cyberpunk-solarpunk-science-fiction-broken.html.

Malzberg, Barry N. "On Engines Again." 1992. *Breakfast in the Ruins*. Baen Books, 2007. 210-15.

——. "On Decadence." 1992. *Breakfast in the Ruins*. Baen Books, 2007. 255-60.

——. "Rage, Pain, Alienation, and Other Aspects of the Writing of Science Fiction." 2005. *Breakfast in the Ruins*. Baen Books, 2007. 195-99.

——. "The Fifties: Recapitulation and Coda." 1979. *Breakfast in the Ruins*. Baen Books, 2007. 52-55.

——. "The Number of the Beast." 1980. *Breakfast in the Ruins*. Baen Books, 2007. 14-17.

——. "The Science Fiction of Science Fiction." 1979. *Breakfast in the Ruins*. Baen Books, 2007. 80-86.

Nicholls, Peter. "New Wave." *The Encyclopedia of Science Fiction*, 2 Apr. 2015, http://www.sf-encyclopedia.com/entry/new_wave.

Pringle, David. *The Ultimate Guide to Science Fiction*. Pharos Books, 1990.

Sterling, Bruce. "Preface." 1986. *Mirrorshades: A Cyberpunk Anthology*. Ace Books, 1988. ix-xvi.

Vonnegut, Kurt. *Breakfast of Champions*. 1973. Dell, 1991.

PROLOGUE

Revelations is a new concept in the media.

Revelations is a stunning look into ourselves.

Through the refinement of the interview-format, brought to a new level through the brilliance of its intensity, Americans of all walks of life, great and small, powerful and oppressed, will expose themselves through a series of searing insights, to their utmost depths.

Revelations, produced and administered by the distinguished Marvin L. Martin, will be the most exciting program of this or any season. We urge you to consult your commitments and time schedules NOW and then communicate with us through the special letterhead number personalized to handle your own account. Time slots in thirty-second, one-minute and two-minute intervals are all available but they are GOING FAST.

This will be the show of the eighties.

I

Gentlemen:

I write to you at this time in this way, not in any real hope that you will be able to use me on your program but because, finally, there is nowhere left to turn. And did not Marvin Martin himself, at the conclusion of the program not three weeks ago, tell us that *Revelations* was a Court of Last Resort for the American People?

Revelations is the only remaining hope, the only outlet now through which I might be able to tell my story . . . the only agency to which I can turn with at least the hope of a hearing.

Let me begin by apologizing for my use of the language which is still sometimes awkward. I come from a technical background and finished only the required courses in college English having, until very recently, no respect for self-expression. Engineers had special courses in English open to them which were largely remedial. I see now how misdirected my life was and have been trying hard to improve my writing for several months but there are still occasional lapses in which I seem illiterate and most of the time I can only strive for a dull, facile style which makes me sound as if I were spelling out the basis for a Manual of

Tools. Inside I am eloquent; I ask you to peer through this clumsiness of syntax to see the man within, impaled upon the cross of his need like a butterfly upon a painful nail.

Let me begin by introducing myself. My name is Walter Monaghan and will make no impression upon you, sadly, although it is a matter of public record that I was the twenty-ninth man on the moon. I was a member of the historic Fifteenth Expedition which in those days received a good deal of coverage from the press even though that coverage, alas, was not what it had been in the happy sixties when the gleaming faces of moon-bound astronauts would leer from newspapers for days and weeks, their wives and noxious children being the subject of many sidebar stories. Those wives! Those children! Never has the case been better made for adultery, promiscuity, divorce and flight than by them although the wives never had the chance, of course, to tell Their Side of the Story.

How loathsome the space program had already become to America by the time of the Fifteenth Expedition! I keep a complete file of all coverage granted us and it was easy to see that by that time the media could barely suppress their revulsion. Now things have become even more terrible; I feel a certain hesitancy in even listing my credentials, I apologize for the program and for myself, gentlemen . . . but it was the assumption that failed and not the men. The men were trapped within it just as I am trapped within the cave of my very poor writing style. They deserve better. Every one of us deserves better, gentlemen; please remember that. Even Marvin Martin concedes, at the end of every program, that the acts revealed are less terrible than the symptoms. Am I right? Do I understand? Do I glean, so to speak, the message of your program?

Biographical details. I must stick to the point; the mind wanders and wavers, the mind is not what it used to be, I have a continual impulse to scream behind this sun-bronzed face. Until my recent discharge (involuntary) from the program, I had spent seven years (seven years!) in the employ of the space agency, moving from the moon to a desk job, making way for younger men, worked my way into one of those pointless liaison jobs which were created for ex-astronauts who got caught in the depression and had nowhere to go but whose continual employment on space flights would have sent senescence speeding out into the dark at seven tottering miles per second. The space agency, one of the most truly monstrous organizations ever enacted by the mad heart of man, does take care of its own. Up to a point. This is not an agency which is truly disloyal and my case against it does not fall on those grounds. I am not a petty complainer.

(Sometime later, at an interview perhaps, I look forward to telling you what became of the thirtieth man on the moon. Also the thirty-fourth and the forty-ninth, to say nothing of the twenty-first. You will be surprised; these details will alter your entire perspective. Embittered I may be but you should hear some of the other case histories.)

Eventually—what span of time, what implication this covers!—problems within the agency forced what is referred to as my "discharge." I had learned a great deal; sitting at a desk unlike parading to the moon gives a man a chance to think and it is possible that I Knew Too Much. Some hint of foreknowledge, a pellet of inference exploded deep within the agency's bureaucracy and I was fired.

Fired! Think of this: it was no ordinary discharge; I was let go with a recommendation so subtly unfavorable that I have been unable to obtain civilian employment of almost any

4

sort (I exclude the occupation of short order cook or memo typist) and am now languishing on the very last of the minimal savings I was able to accumulate during my time in the agency. I calculate food expenses, argue with the landlord of these furnished rooms for small concessions in rent, burn papers in the fireplace to hold down heating expenses. (The landlord provides none.) This is not a respectable kind of life for a thirty-three year old ex-astronaut; fortunately, my wife, who abandoned me without forwarding address, has made no demands for severance. My wife, although a nice person in many ways, never contributed to the household economically although the contraception she insisted upon using was so stunningly effective that I can only now bless her. Despite the battery of equipment she would take to the bed, making it look sometimes like a small trench during close combat. As you see, I am not unappreciative of her.

I am a tortured man. Monaghan is a tortured man. My prose, elevated and depressed by turns, perceptive and imperceptive, obsessed and detached, a jumble of the highest rhetoric and the low, is good indication of this state. So is my typing which I can see is rather bizarre even for this old machine. I am haunted now all of the time by dim thrashings within the reservoirs of guilt; now my conscience itself, sighing familiarly, begs to tell all. "Tell all, Monaghan, let the poisons out!" my conscience (an old enemy) shrieks and I am willing, I am willing. The corruption of the agency; its madness and the things that it forces people to do must be known by "the public." When "the public" finally understands this there will be an explosion and scandal utterly unlike any other in the history of this unhappy country. I have staggered into an uneasy populism, as you see (I believe in The People, their common sense, their shrewd, suspicious wisdom); also, I do not believe that this can go on forever. The agency cannot get away with it.

(The secret of the agency has not been revealed to date—I hasten to answer your inevitable question—because those who know it either profit by that knowledge or like myself until recently are incapable of speech.)

A brief and embarrassed admission. In recent weeks I have tried to interest some of the following in my story: publishers, lawyers, agents, weekly news magazines, veteran's groups and the Joint Commission on Human Rights. Only form responses or silence have ensued. Maybe I am thinking of fear or bureaucratic indifference; perhaps it is my rather lunatic style which discourages credibility. Whatever the reason, I have been treated in cavalier fashion. It is difficult to retain one's faith in the face of such abuse. Nevertheless I will not yield. No man who has trodden the surface of the moon (which has the aspect of nothing more sensational than an untended sandbox) can discourage easily.

I WILL NOT YIELD. (I capitalize this, not knowing how to make italics on typescript.) I feel that it is my mission to tell the truth, a mission which contains a faint spark of the divine. (But I am no religious fanatic; only a man who has been trapped in lies for seven years. This explains my mad sense of earnestness like a confidant on the subway dipping his hand into your pocket for a coin while the other, with flourishes, details the Story of His Life.)

I appeal. I appeal to your program. I appeal to "Revelations." Within the context of your format I will tell the Full Story of the agency subject to any limitations which you would care to impose. This must be divulged. The agency must be exposed. As one who is aware however of your format—

As one who is aware of your format (I watch much television in these ancient rooms; my wife's last gift to me upon her abandonment was this old color set whose beneficent rays doubtless strike cancer into my very bones as I sit poised before it, tuning into America) I realize that this material may not be quite proper for your program which instead seeks admissions of a somewhat more personal nature.

So I make the following proposal: I will comply with your format. If I am given the chance, one chance, to put my facts before The People I would have no objection to discussing my: a) sex life or b) personal habits or c) intimate details of my marriage or d) certain sex perversities of my youth (so obscure that not even the agency's security check turned them up, so private that not even my hands remember them) as long as these areas of discussion do not preclude my imparting that basic information I want to give. Which is about the agency and what they have done to people. That information is of greatest significance but I am willing to wrap it in a blanket of personal disaster and shame.

Naturally I am willing to accept full responsibility for any and all of my disclosures and I will sign any waivers that will please in order to release you from potential damages and to keep your legal department happy. (I figure you must have an enormous legal department.)

May I be given then the chance to talk with one of your staff? (You must have a very large staff.) I know that I can prove to his satisfaction and to yours that I am serious and that what I have to say is of the most crucial importance. Perhaps this letter is hopeless, perhaps I am once again writing only to myself. Perhaps it will be discarded along with the tens of other such letters you receive every day. But I retain the belief—

—Well, I retain the belief that our institutions are not completely hopeless and that they can be changed, that the individual voice has not yet been squeezed out forever. I contemplate drastic actions if I am not heard—there is no paralysis of will HERE, gentlemen!—but will give the principles of Vox Populi One Last Chance.

II

To Hurwitz: Well, it does check out. Someone with this name, anyway, was on the moon a few years ago. We checked out the clips. Taciturn, low-profile, the sidebar stories began referring to him as "the silent astronaut" (for *silent* read *dull*). Amazing how all this goes out of mind. It all reeks of a gentler time. Whatever happened to the moon? Now manned space stations are the ticket.

His wife: pretty woman (at least in the photos), distracted manner, had her hands in her hair a lot. "Walter always wanted to go to the furthest spaces; now he has his dream." Standard wifely crap. Maybe she blew under all the pressure. Couldn't blame her.

I don't think that there's anything here. Pretty routine stuff and despite Monaghan's bravura assurances, no one I know seems to give a shit about the space program any more. Manned space stations? Only to watch China. But the personal habits and recriminations of these monkeys just can't be packaged in today's market. Too little personality. Old archaic symptoms of repression and authoritarianism and how are you going to sell that these days? Could repression be the coming thing?

On the other hand, there is a certain wistful note of appeal which caught the reader. The reader is only twenty-three years old (twenty-three! do you remember when we were twenty-three?) and takes her job seriously. Also she takes *me* seriously and has large breasts. I do the best I can. In the office, however, I am all business.

Perhaps jaded types you know would have the wrong slant on this. Maybe there is something here although you'd have to approach it from cross-angles. Maybe you could sell him as an anti-astronautics astronaut although this stuff too has been done.

Do you want us to pursue it?

III

Fuck it. I've got enough creeps already.

IV

I've been in the business too long. That is all it is; I've been in the business too long and I can no longer force myself to believe any of this. In different circumstances I could resign and look for something respectable but it is too late, Hurwitz is forty-two years old, Hurwitz is declining, these sieges of resolve come further and further apart now and feel only like the last twitches of the damned. Hurwitz is confident: querulousness has been banished by Hurwitz. I know what I was, what I am, what I will become, what waits for me. The only salvation is in that recognition. Remember that.

There are limits to this situation. I see that now. It has been overspent, squeezed dry and one cannot, even a Hurwitz, eternally produce. There must be an end to all of this; there is a law like gold which glints from the center of anything like this and that law is: *three years*. With luck, with a shakeup at the fringes maybe four, but never five. Never.

You can ride the wind only so far before it dashes you to emptiness. How philosophical Hurwitz has become! How metaphysical! Would this cosmic resignation have been dreamed when it all began?

I can't get out.

They won't let me out; I won't let *myself* out. Not any more. That was two years ago, the trying. I learned then where I stood in this business, what *Revelations* had made me. There is a fine moral overcast to this business which comes into play when you deal with your competition. Your competition is, perhaps, to be judged more harshly than necessary. Maybe not. Maybe the people I begged for a job two years ago felt that Hurwitz was *better* than *Revelations*; that he had *lowered* himself, that he must now pay the penalty.

For whatever reason, there will be no resignations. I am linked to this nightmare until it collapses. A resignation would be *deus ex machina* and Hurwitz learned early in the game to finish, always finish, what he was doing. In the meantime, I have a job to do.

Discovery. I must find more personalities, more citizens, more possibilities, more biography to place in the hands of Marvin Martin. Who will skewer some and toss back the rest to Hurwitz as unsatisfactory. Until recently I thought the man was insane. This was convenient; it enabled a distancing factor. I talked about "the committed lunacy of a man who can reduce everyone to abstractions." This no longer works. I do not believe that Marvin Martin is insane. I believe something much worse: that the man is serious. He believes in what he is doing. His rage at Hurwitz boils because Hurwitz is failing him in the effort to demolish every single person in the United States of America. The people I give him, if they are not satisfactory, cannot possibly be Americans.

He believes everything and that is the key to the man. *Revelations* is serious. Its purposes are sociological. Confession is catharsis. Uplift brassieres never lie. Blondes have more fun. Three hundred and eighty horses under the hood never fail in acceleration. The market for residuals has not even been tapped. And so on.

Marvin Martin is a highly sentimental man; he dismembers people only out of disenchantment but is still looking for the Next Case that will have no deception to the core. Three years it took me to arrive at this insight, perilously achieved and dangerous in the understanding. Was it worth the trouble?

Meanwhile, it becomes worse and worse. There is no way that it could get any better; the Hurwitz Higher Centers understand this, not with the law glinting golden in the night. State the law for the populace, Hurwitz; in a different time you wrote it up for a master's thesis and had you kept it in mind at the beginning rather than the end you would be in a better condition, my friend: THE ORIGINAL IMPETUS WILL CARRY YOU MIDWAY INTO THE THIRD SEASON BUT NEVER BEYOND. Through the third season the format must either be radically changed or die but since it is the format that took you that far and locks you into the ratings you have, you cannot play with it. You can only hold on to a diminishing, increasing restless audience which does not understand why life is not so much fun any more.

And you go under.

They all go under sooner or later: the modal point is about two and a half years. The freaks that go on for a decade turn out never to have been that strongly programmed in the first place; they snuck on through a series of breaks (because only strongly programmed stuff can for the most part get through) and then were able to work on the format as they went along. They could have been anything at all. They still might be. Besides, Marvin Martin does not believe in rusticity or vaudeville.

Monolithic. Impenetrable. (Hurwitz has a certain low gift for words if not language.) All of it is so classically defined; so this is what it feels like to live in a master's thesis. The law has snatched us; we are in the grip of the law, it is only a matter of a little time until our shrinking ratings collapse completely and in the meantime the spring meetings will have bumped us. Already there are foreshadowings from the network; spring approaches, they wonder about our ideas, they are not pleased with some of the latest ideas and are our plans the same? Do we think that a skull session would be in order or possibly a rethinking of roles? The spring meetings vault upon us like a maddened high jumper on the moon; network will call us in for a conference next week or definitely by February. March at the latest. Some of our calls have not been returned; we are told that there is trouble on the switchboard.

In the meanwhile. In the meanwhile, however, I, Hurwitz, Michael Hurwitz that is to say, Michael Hurwitz must produce. Must produce Michael Hurwitz. Produce. Must. Come. Up. With. Ideas. How did I ever get into this business?

The Hurwitz wife goes south for an extended vacation to think things out. She divorces, she remarries, she is hardly missed. Hurwitz has been out of touch, he is not so sure any more about relationships. Deadly tension around the familiar Hurwitz eyes, a clattering twitch in the area of the left nostril, a hint of monomania in the speech. Autism, neurasthenia. A clear declension in sexual performance, a lack of true invention; now and then (how painful it is to say this) a touch, just a faint whisk as if from the corridors of Belteguese, of psychic impotence. Like a shuddering in the temple, gone and forgotten. Still, the rhythms break. They come askew. Fortunately, I have an understanding staff who are aware of the occupational disease. All applicants are carefully screened for me.

Hurwitz is gaining weight. Last week, I weighed two hundred and thirty-nine pounds on the bathroom scale. The attire was full and attaché case was in hand (I always do this to have a favorable excuse) but nevertheless, I weighed forty pounds less this way only a year ago. I am five feet eleven inches tall when I extend myself. Unextended I am five feet eight.

Hurwitz wrote a master's thesis, Hurwitz is no fool. Obviously there is no way out. Like everyone here except Marvin Martin himself (who is extremely diversified and deep into construction) I am on a one-way ticket. Which way? And where are the skills transferable? There are very few whorehouses left in the world; not one of them to my knowledge now needs an orderly.

V

ANNOUNCER: Good evening. Welcome once again to *Revelations* where the mystery is at last made flesh and where you may see America through the inner lives of its people as America has become. Your host is Marvin Martin. Here is Marvin Martin.

MARTIN: Welcome once again to *Revelations*. My first guest tonight is Doris Jensen of New Capital, Nebraska. Mrs. Jensen—we will call her Doris—is twenty-five years old. She is married, the mother of two children and the wife of a civil-service worker in an armaments division of a government subcontractor which will be nameless. Remember the aspect of civil service, this is important. Doris completed two years at the University of Nebraska before quitting midway in her junior year to marry. She now sees her primary activities as those of "homemaker" and "secretary of the local parent-teacher's organization." Her hobbies, she states, are freelance writing and embroidery and her physical attractiveness more or less speaks for itself. As you see. Good evening, Doris. Are you ready for some revelations?

MRS. JENSEN: Good evening. I'm very nervous right now. I know that maybe I shouldn't be but—

MARTIN: Are you wearing pair of falsies underneath that sweater of yours, Doris? Or are we supposed to believe that that angle is real?

MRS. JENSEN: They, uh, they're real. They told me that it would be like this but I didn't think it would start so fast, uh—

MARTIN: It's all yours then; is that what you and the brassiere want us to believe?

MRS. JENSEN: I'm just so nervous. (Giggles.) Maybe this is the wrong thing to say, about being nervous, you know, but—

MARTIN: Why?

MRS. JENSEN: Why what?

MARTIN: Come to the point, Doris. Stay with it, swing with me, let it work. It can work if you just stay with it. Come right back on the questions quick; first thing that comes into your mind. Why are you nervous?

MRS. JENSEN: That question you asked me.

MARTIN: Just warmup.

MRS. JENSEN: I guess I'm afraid of what you're going to do to me. I mean, I know what happens here; how couldn't I? I've watched the program dozens of times and I tried to be prepared but . . . well, to tell you the truth, it's entirely different when you're finally on. And there's really no preparation, is there? I know that things can get, well, kind of rough—

MARTIN: It's not what we do to you. It's what you do to yourself. Stop being so defensive. Come on, relax, I hate to do retapes.

MRS. JENSEN: I don't think I understand. What do you mean, do to myself?

MARTIN: That's the central part. The rest is nonsense. Now hold on there and we'll be back in just a moment.

MRS. JENSEN: (Indistinguishable.)

(*Insert. Precision Industries, thirty-second tape. Cola Products, thirty-second tape. Stampler's Commune, one-minute tape. Tracking from network. Hold for verify.*)

MARTIN: Ah. And back again.

MRS. JENSEN: I know.

MARTIN: Just the two of us conversing. Think of it as a private conversation between strangers; the confrontations which can occur on a cross-country bus in the hush of night.

MRS. JENSEN: Oh. Bus rides.

MARTIN: In a small space, exchanging confidences. Consider the audience the anonymous sleeping passengers on the bus; heedless they rush into the night together and yet apart from us. Please tell me if you will about your first sexual experience, Doris. I do like to call you Doris; it fits you.

MRS. JENSEN: Oh yes. Doris. (Pause.)

MARTIN: We're waiting, Doris. I'm waiting.

MRS. JENSEN: Well, what? Waiting for what? Do you want to know with who? Or when? Or what it was like or stuff like that?

MARTIN: Everything.

MRS. JENSEN: Oh.

MARTIN: Everything. Let's move in bit by bit, and start with the chronological. When did you first have sexual intercourse?

MRS. JENSEN: I'm trying to think. I'm trying, I really am, please let me. I guess that it must have been at the University.

MARTIN: You mean you can't really place it in time, Doris? That's unusual.

MRS. JENSEN: I didn't say I couldn't place it, I'm just nervous!

MARTIN: How old were you?

MRS. JENSEN: That would be, uh, in my sophomore year. I was twenty. No, I guess I was nineteen. Must we go into all of this? I was a sophomore.

MARTIN: This vagueness hints real stress. Probe this canker; let the insights flow. Was it with a male?

MRS. JENSEN: A man! It was with a man! Paul, my husband. Paul was the only man who I ever . . . listen (pause) I don't want to do this. Really, Mr. Martin, I just can't do this any more.

MARTIN: Relax, Doris. These little tensions mean nothing; from them the truths emerge and the truths are as high, pristine, lucid and detached as if they came from the mouths of angels. We are only the medium toward discovery.

MRS. JENSEN: What?

MARTIN: Now be explicit. I want details.

MRS. JENSEN: Details?

MARTIN: I said that already!

MRS. JENSEN: Well, I can't. I just can't. I can't do stuff like that, I'm sorry.

MARTIN: Why not?

MRS. JENSEN: Because I can't. I just don't want to. I know that this is a big break and that there's money in it. I know about that agreement I signed before I even was interviewed but I just can't. I won't do it any more and you've got to realize—

MARTIN: Doris. *Doris.* We were talking about your first sexual experience. With Paul, you say, this man who became your husband. If you would please continue it would be much easier for all of us. These technicians are already on triple-time.

MRS. JENSEN: Continue. (Pause.)

MARTIN: Well?

MRS. JENSEN: No. I—uh . . . no, I won't do it. I know that we need the money and I signed that agreement but I just can't. *I can't do it.* I applied for the program and went through the whole thing but I was wrong. I made a mistake, that's all. Didn't you ever make a mistake? I have no impression of your humanity.

MARTIN: My patience is ever so slightly tried now. Just a shade.

MRS. JENSEN: Please let me alone. I won't say any more about this. I want to stop.

MARTIN: I don't like your attitude, Doris. In fact, I am losing my temper.

MRS. JENSEN: Well, don't be that way.

MARTIN: I try to be a temperate man but sometimes I wonder. Do I have to kill another taping?

MRS. JENSEN: Mr. Martin, I made a terrible mistake. I admit that and I apologize to everyone; I apologize to you. I won't take any of the money and I'll do anything you say but I just can't. I can't go into all of my private experiences. I'm twenty-five years old and already in a lot of trouble and my experiences are maybe the only thing that I'll have left. To make me—

MARTIN: Doris, this is a show. It is a professional presentation which involves you only marginally. We are in the studios and we are taping.

MRS. JENSEN: You're always interrupting me. And that's another thing. Why can't you ever let people finish a sentence? I noticed that; you never do. You just manipulate people and make them do things for what you want and I can't take this any more! I told you, I know that I made a horrible mistake and that I shouldn't have gotten involved. It was just that we're always short of money and we got to thinking how could we raise some money and just for a lark I thought I'd apply and then you got me an agent and put me through all those tests and so on but I never *thought* about it. I never realized what was going to happen, I just kept on pushing that out of my mind and no one really prepared me although I should have known from watching the program. But I can't push it away any more. I won't tell you my experiences and private thoughts; it's evil.

MARTIN: I'm not interrupting you see.

MRS. JENSEN: And now that you've finally given me a chance to say something I want to say this: I think it's sick. Your whole program is sick, that's what it is. You're playing on the worst in people, their worst possibilities, their need to find ugliness and it's just like a man on the subway poking and prying in the dark.

MARTIN: That's bad metaphor, Doris.

MRS. JENSEN: Don't you tell me about metaphor! I don't have to take this.

MARTIN: I think I know what's going on here. In fact, I know exactly what's going on here.

MRS. JENSEN: It's vicious! To put people on television and probe at their secrets. Now I think it's just a symbol of what is happening to this country, what we've allowed ourselves to become.

MARTIN: You've done very well, Doris. That's quite enough now.

MRS. JENSEN: But your time is finished! This program will never survive into another season. You see, I *know*—

MARTIN: Let's kill the tape now.

MRS. JENSEN: I have in my pocket a letter from the President of the Committee for the Refurbishment, a statement, really—

MARTIN: Is the tape off yet?

MRS. JENSEN: Parasites nibbling at people but the Committee has now determined— (Tape ends.)

VI

Oh my God. Oh my God.

VII

Get that son of a bitch Hurwitz and get rid of him before I start thinking personally about him. This is an order.

VIII

If given a chance I know that I can explain this. Please give me that chance.

IX

To Hurwitz: No sir. I am not interested.

My capacity is merely to pass down the line and I have been advised to tell you that your services remain terminated as of the coming Friday.

You let this ringer through. The screening process is your responsibility. Any explanations you would offer on this fiasco are utterly beside the point.

Records indicate that you interviewed this woman on March 11, 197–, either personally or by proxy and signed a statement as follows:

> Doris Jensen will be one of the most remarkable participants which *Revelations* has had to date (sic). She is highly recommended: she combines seeming openness and vulnerability with the capacity to make the most shocking and graphic sexual admissions. These admissions have been made in the interview with great detail. The contrast between her mannerisms and the content of her speech is extraordinarily prurient and will make a most rewarding segment, we feel. She is therefore approved for taping. Agency procedures and releases have been ordered. It is suggested that standard fees apply. (March 14, 197–)

Fifteen minutes of valuable taping time were then wasted upon this advocate of repression from the Committee for Refurbishment. (To say nothing of the hours of preparation procedures; the coding, the organization.) The taping schedule was almost destroyed and I have been asked to remind you that it was only through a combination of extraordinary luck and timing that the second available participant had enough undisclosed data in his background (due to your very poor interviewing procedures) to fill the entire span of the show.

Otherwise, we would have had to cancel taping and run yet another repeat. *We cannot take this.* Even so, it will be one of our most disastrous editions—William Sommers, whether or not he sat in Congress for a term many years ago, is nothing but a common drunk and fag, stuff which we have featured many times before and can continue to no good purpose.

THE SHOW IS NOT BUILDING. THE SHOW IS NOT GROWING.

(I remind you that your memo on Sommers referred to *him* as an "exciting possibility . . . since he has had associations with many major politicians." *What politicians?* The man allows to spending two congressional years in confinement in a hotel room, drinking himself into reactionary legislation.) What kind of ratings do you think that we're going to pick up on this one?

Hurwitz, you are totally responsible for Doris Jensen's appearance on the program. That subordinates or collaborators might have sneaked this one through you is no defense. *You* were responsible for your staff. (But no more, no more; autonomy in the screening division has been abolished.) It seems to us that you have lost personal and professional control. Perhaps some time in a good, private institution might be advisable. Perhaps a rest and change of scenery will do you well; there is no reason for you to carry these heavy responsibilities eternally, now you can put the burdens down. We will help you to put those burdens down by blacklisting you through every corner of the industry.

X

Gentlemen:

Reference is made to my recent letter. Have you received it? Please do not feel that I am rushing you for a reply but I would like some brief acknowledgment of receipt but take all the time you want and, of course, if an acknowledgment would be too much trouble for you don't bother with that either; the important thing is to know that I am at last getting a fair hearing.

XI

I found the bitch in the west nineties. She was tucked in there so neatly that they could have used a lever.

But it was easy. Sometimes, everything is easy. She had another name and a different kind of wardrobe, but the Service nailed her to ground in less than six hours after I put in the call. Of course I had to pay the tab out of pocket; the Service is expensive, and not a credit operation.

Hurwitz long since arrived at this insight: the compression of his part of the world is phenomenal. There are very few of us in the media game and most of us, it seems, grew up together or have appointments to make. No surprises. Nothing is a surprise any more, Hurwitz being a completely disenchanted man. I might have figured her for a little further uptown, that was all.

So I went there. No preliminaries, no preparation; two cold drinks in readiness but purely mechanical, ritual in nature, less for the head than the intestines. She was up there surrounded by prints on the walls and bay windows; four stories, a walk-up. Scuttling of rats on the perimeter; held in bay by the apartment itself. Fairly impressive. I said everything that I had to say and then, having transferred the account, so to speak, Hurwitz permitted himself to relax for the first time in three days or maybe four and sat on the foul, flowered couch facing a large mirror, watching the knowledge dance and illumine his eyes; the high, intense cheekbones of the familiar Hurwitz face tight with assurance as I could see it sink into her.

"That's what happened," I said.

"I'm sorry." She shifted on the chair opposite, seemed to look at me, finally did not, broke the glance to turn and look out the window, observe the West 93rd Street panorama which included the guarded car that I had parked outside, my own private, personal guard sitting in the rear seat playing incuriously with some armaments. (All cautions about West 93rd Street are true but it is possible to tuck people away there, even today.) "I told you that already. I'm terribly sorry and you know I am so how many times do you want me to say it? I didn't know that it was going to lead to anything like that; I didn't even think to tell you the truth that I'd *get* on the program. I expected to be bumped out, right after the preliminary interview. I didn't even *expect* an interview. It was just a try, they told me and how did I know what they were really after? I'm embarrassed. But what can I say beyond that, Mr. Hurwitz? That I should kill myself? The whole thing just got away from me, that's all; it wasn't anything personal."

The rhetoric. The rhetoric was different from that on the taping, likewise the skin tone and the angle of the breasts which had narrowed considerably to a more yielding, if disappointing softness. I could see myself touching and twirling those breasts now and it was a disappointment, it was not what I had had in mind, it had been her gorgeous, insane unassailability which I had desired (shades of High School, Hurwitz!) and now she was different, she was open, she looked like every woman you had passed on the street and known you could, in certain circumstances, have fucked her; the waste of sex was already in her. "I don't believe it," I said, out of the center of all this insight. "I don't believe any of it."

"You'll have to," the woman I might have fucked (could yet fuck) said, "because that's the truth."

A dictum. Hurwitz interrupts his recollections to give an addendum to future generations who will run and scamper down the humble paths staggered on by Hurwitz: there are no Refurbishment Committee fanatics living undiscovered in Omaha. Living undiscovered in New York. No embittered reactionaries frozen into social security and sexual fear in the provinces. No native-born singers of the land hitting guitars unheard in the midwest. None of these people now exist. They all have agents and were cornered by the Interested a long time ago, were brought into the central agency to be packaged and farmed out. The last true revivalist preacher went to Allied Famous in 1954. The last college-educated whore was signed by Golden in 1961. The last preventative war advocate cast his lot with the Maller Associates in 1973. Since then, we have all been making casting calls and generally scrambling. Allied Famous, however, retains the inside track.

"That's not enough," Hurwitz said, adopting a formal and rather threatening tone, distancing himself from that glinting mirror of neuroses in which all of his more ambitious gestures seemed to be reflected. Someday we will have to get to the root of this. "I don't want any more of your cheap explanations or apologies. You fucked us badly and you'll pay for it." A certain bluntness in this business is often salutary.

She backed away, quailed slightly. "I don't want to hear that language," she said. "Take it back to the time when you grew up. It makes no impression."

"Listen, lady," I said, "if you must know, my instincts are all to beating you up. I'd like to get physical with you in no attentive way. But I've been in the acquisitions business too long; I look on everything as a package. It's difficult to get up the personal interest to smash any more. Nevertheless, do not prod me. I am fat and out of condition but I have resources."

She said nothing, leaned back on the couch. Her attitude shifted subtly; she seemed to be testing a set of reactions. "You talk interestingly," she said.

"You went through all of the preliminary investigations, the interviews, the preparations, without a murmur. Not an indication," I said, "not an indication of what you had in mind. You tested out perfectly. A real professional. The waivers were in order, the forms, the husband's co-signature, the works. A verification from the city of Omaha. Releases. Agency contract. So you got in."

"I never expected to."

"Hear me out. Hurwitz is preparing a line of reasoning; do not interrupt him. You get in. You get by the process and on the platform and you spiel Marvin Martin. Rendering incendiary our purposes. Holding our deficiencies up to scrutiny. Meddling with the Hurwitz career which is no feat of engineering, I assure you. Causing Marvin Martin worry and distress. It's all too purposeful."

"Purposeful?"

"You're no dupe, baby. It doesn't sing. This whole thing was planned."

"They roped me in," she said. "You'll have to believe that none of it was really my idea. You're a smart man and you figured out a lot but maybe because of your business you read motives where there aren't any. I was only doing what I was supposed to."

She crossed and uncrossed her rather hard legs on the couch, reached for a cigarette. All of them, in and out of the business, are always reaching for cigarettes or glasses or something; like characters in bad novels they have no sense of timing or space. "I have no convictions about this one way or the other," she said. "It was just a job to do; I was hired, in fact. There was a whole application and interview. I had to do a job, didn't I? I needed the money. Try to put yourself in my position. You *are* in my position, you know."

"You got cool," I said. "You have a certain self-possession, a high patina of gloss we like to call it in the Bensonhurst Flats which incidentally I came from. You're probably even a fair lay, I've decided that and I'm surprised that you're still scrounging around for this kind of business. You're over the hill now and if you're as good as you look, you're well beyond this. This isn't your kind of thing at all; I don't think you're over the hill. Something stinks here; the whole situation."

I stood, moved over to her, let the Hurwitz bulk rest imposingly on the couch and stared. There are advantages to obesity (a cycle I have been in and out at least ten times in my life; every gain a loss, every loss an understanding, every understanding a reduction, every reduction a gain) which are tightly linked to the smaller virtues of fear. She squirmed under the intent Hurwitz gaze: a compact tense bitch this one, a slight sloppiness around the edges purely enticing, legs glinting golden as a Law, the cheat on the breasts a little disturbing but still not too much wrong with them, a new slash of knowledge knifing across the cheekbones. She broke the cigarette and put it into the ashtray unlit. "Stop that," she said, the voice rising a little. "Now just cut that out and leave me alone. You're making no impression on me at all anyway."

"I got it," I said. "I figured the whole thing out. You're no employee. You come direct."

"Direct?"

"Direct from the competition. Don't ask what competition yet; I'm still working on that. They figured to give it a try, nothing to lose and anyway there's always some Committee for Refurbishment hanging around. You can pin the whole thing on the Committee."

"I want you to leave now, Mr. Hurwitz. We have nothing more to say to each other. Everything you want to hear you can tell yourself."

"They wouldn't risk a freelancer for something like this. No, stay with me; it's very interesting to see how it works out. I wouldn't be surprised if you came from the very top. The upper levels. It depends on who we're murdering the most, that's all. The thing is that I was stupid. That's not forgivable, even in my business. You can't get away with being stupid. Hurwitz pays. Hurwitz pays the price for his arrogance. But he is still on the trail of fools."

"Get out of here," she said. She twisted the legs, the breasts bounced. Fairly titillating; old memories from the Hurwitz racial unconsciousness burbled. About ten years fell from her and I saw that she was thirty-eight, maybe older than that. Her eyes started refocusing at a level of mad intensity, a trait with which I am familiar. It has happened to me. The shape of her face changed; she snorted.

"All of it falling into place," I said. "How neat, how good it feels. You're a perfect prototype. The best. A hard, sensual bitch hinting at a whiff of the sexual goods. That's always fine; that's the first level. That can be picked right up, no belief in subtleties. Then come over with some fanatic hype.

Committee for the Refurbishment. That drives through the second level and then confess that you were a ringer for those freaks. Third level by then. Three levels of connection. Clever. Well done. Somebody is really thinking over there; thinking on the Hurwitz level. But Hurwitz has another card. Not for nothing has he been in the Bensonhurst school system. You don't have a fourth level, do you bitch? I know the type. Prong far enough down—or up—and there are no levels left. I've known some though that took seven or eight so you're not really such hot stuff. I know you. You get all loose toward the end, the rhythms break, the fluids get dry. Your hips collapse and the thighs lose momentum, over and out. Back and forth. Cunt."

"I don't have to take this." She backed slightly on the couch, using the still-good thighs to generate heat in the motion. "You don't do this to me. They already put me through too much. It's too much; the price is too high. Get out of here."

"They took a big chance, though, putting through a leader like you. A loss leader, huh? I bet the axe was singing and you didn't even know it. Betting that they could get you through all the hurdles, knowing what the odds would be and so on. But you've got talent. On the high executive level there's always talent, don't miss it, hunt for it and it's there. You did well. It wasn't such a long shot then, you figured."

"Nothing. Nothing."

"You think you're getting a promotion but I bet they knock you out in six to eight months. They'll set you up and then pass you over and you'll have to resign. I know. I've been that way. Of course you might have another bonus in mind altogether; maybe you get your promotions from a different angle toward the ceiling."

"You disgusting bastard," she said, getting elemental finally and not a moment too soon, "you fat son of a bitch, you miserable speculator, you *broker*, you manipulator, hooking them in with your lies so that that monster can open them up and spill them out and all in the glorification of *fraud*, well let me tell you something because I'll lay it on the line, why not, I'll just—"

"Oh Doris Jensen," I said and seized her wrist, "that is, whatever your name really is but we won't worry about that now and I've gotten kind of fond of Doris Jensen, it fits you so very well, oh Doris Jensen, don't make speeches to me, don't ruin it," and twisted the lovely wrist, twisted it abruptly, brought her through pain into shocking connection (I knew she was the type) and as all the smoothness fled from her face she looked older yet, older and older Doris Jensen, maybe forty-five now and fading fast and I could see all of the little animals of her past begin to parade from the face, flutter into the room, "ah, Doris Jensen, don't talk, don't ruin our new relationship that way; let Hurwitz do all the talking because he does it so nicely. This is his business. Oh, you got Hurwitz into bad trouble, very bad trouble for Hurwitz who is a close friend of mine and this is not so good because Hurwitz does not like trouble. Hurwitz is not paid a huge salary which he cannot manage to be made a fool of. There are too many responsibilities, too much history, too many complications and too high the stake for error. I looked up everything, you bitch. Everything. Don't you think they know?"

"No you didn't."

"Oh yes I did. I got it all down on paper, not that I would bring paper into this neighborhood or anything else personal."

"You couldn't. They assured me—"

"They assured you of nothing. Don't you think that they can lie too? I got everything; I spread some money around and what do you think the cost is to get hold of anything in this business? It's a money business, it's only money. A hundred? Maybe a thousand? For ten thousand dollars I can tell you who the president was fucking last night if he fucked at all, not being privy to his preferences right now. You go right down to the sources. The sources are all at the bottom mucking around; you toss in the fishing pole, you pull out the information and *hook in*. For a hundred thousand I'll find out what Kennedy dreamed for us when he was shot. You used to be a little bit of an actress, didn't you? That too in the background. You weren't too damned good; the game knocked you out in less than a year but at the university theatre level you showed a little capacity. Cabaret stuff. Bits, improvisations. A little patter, a little dirt. So they knew you knew. What's the price, Doris Jensen? I love that name Doris Jensen and I'll always call you that in my heart."

"Bastard. Bastard."

"Ah yes," I said, bringing the wrist all the way behind her but tenderly, not wanting to hurt, only a whisk of authority; only tenderness now. I loved her. "Tell me," I said, "are they giving you the whips for that one? Or am I thinking of something less exotic."

"I hate you."

"Cunt," I said. "Cunt, I love you. I love you! I see your cunt now. Beautiful; your beautiful . . . why couldn't you have made it simple?"

And it all fell away from her then. The hatred, the posture, even the angle of the breasts. Where there had been one thing, there was another. Or nothing, an absolute blank. Abstraction, the blanding of affect. At the center, like all the rest of them, this was her secret: she contained nothing.

(I am no exception. Inside all of these postures Hurwitz is empty, empty, clicking machinery at rest. This realization came to me a long time ago. That is why I put such high credence on devices. All the devices.)

"I was promised," she said, "I was promised that there would be no follow up. We thought that we could get away with it. I was convinced it was a lock. We didn't see this at all."

"Not we. Stop thinking *we*. You were the implement. All the time it was *they*."

"No one thought—"

Hurwitz is a desperate man. He has very high expenses which already he cannot meet. This they didn't include; they didn't reckon with that at all. Don't you see it now, cunt, they lied to you too. They did the same thing to you that they did to us."

"They couldn't."

"Oh, yes, they could. They knew you too well. They had their reasons, they always have reasons and it was worth the price. You're an employee. They hired you for the job."

"Oh God."

"To shoot this gap, one big price. Oh, how they must hate! Who would have known?"

"Pain," she said. "The pain—"

"What was the price? Hurwitz is curious; now he can ask you anything. The formalities are over. What was the price on it?"

She groaned and tried to move away; then collapsed in submission, rubbing her head against a Hurwitz knee. Strange, fluid warmth moving in uneven waves. "Authority," she said. "There was a package I wanted. I could have brought it out too; it would have worked. It was in their interests. But they wanted this done anyway."

"Just that."

"Maybe a bonus."

"A little bonus."

"It wasn't discussed."

"That would figure. That would be the key: who cares about packaging anyway, right?"

"All right," she said. "Don't hurt me any more. I'll go down right there with you and tell them the whole story. Anything you want. I'm tired, too tired, I can't stand pain any more. I'll sign anything you want. Releases. Blanks. Just leave me be."

"In due course," I said. And let her go. A momentary feeling of accomplishment vaulted through me drunkenly, airy disconnection, then, on its heels, the same old despair slunk in wearing clown costume, clambering madly through the ladders, snickering, waving cap with bells.

Because it never ends. Nothing ever ends. It is all dryly, mechanically predictable and it leads nowhere at all. Hurwitz understands this. This is part of his living, recognizing that what is always carried around cannot be removed. The price is too high.

"You'll do all of that when I'm ready," I said. "Right now I have no time for releases, forms. Paperwork is not the answer. No tolerance for paperwork. We'll wait on that just a while."

"And now?" she said. "And now?"

But the arch of her body was already the answer. We were in the same business; she knew the technique of summation, what Hurwitz would take to balance the accounts. I could feel how she would be, the arch, the slackness, forty-five years of Doris Jensen damp against me: damp, the tremblings of her body sheer gesture, just a mask, which would collapse against Hurwitz into a wet, oozing vacuity all dough and darkness beneath. Good, ah God it would be good, it would be just what I had wanted; it was what I had come here to take. She sobbed against me, lifted, trembled. "Just that?" she said, knowing. "Just that? That's the only thing you want? Only this?"

"Oh, no," I said. "There's more. But the rest of it we can pick up later. Later."

And laid her then right down the floor. Hauled up her skirt for entry, pulled down her pants, nothing else; no connection with the sinking, vanished breasts, no touch on the hard lips, the clammy hands. Simple, hard, driving contact on the rug as Hurwitz took out his measure upon her (his psychic impotence forgotten; Hurwitz has a sense of Occasion), meeting her darkness with floods of pure Hurwitzian slime which rocked into her alley like thieves stumbling toward light, fleeing the law. "Cunt," I said, "cunt, bitch, ugly, frozen bitch," and bit her, and she laughed in an ear and brought her thighs down against me. Clamping, jamming, moving me up. I had been wrong about the softness. Her thighs did not go soft.

But still, past the climax, no end to it. Woe, diminution and the sense of banishment. A hint of beseechment in my gestures as I scrambled away from her.

So much then: so much for Sutton Place.

XII

Yes, I am frightened. Yes, fright is the conditioner, the center of it; it is impossible, even at the moment of assault not to know that easy, palpitating fear that is the center of the dilemma. The fear I know; it is the hard, smooth knife-edge of it, skewering all the parts that I cannot stand; the capacity of terror to split apart. Could have hurt her terribly, I could; could have left her shrieking on the floor, begging for necessity, yet knew within the Hurwitz channels as I left her only the frantic scurryings of the frantic heart, oozing its frail damp . . . peace, Hurwitz, peace.

XIII

Gentlemen:

I am still waiting for a reply and trying to be patient but some acknowledgment, even a postcard or one-line memo would be helpful because I think I am entitled to it; now just try to consider if you will.

XIV

To Hurwitz: Previous memoranda on this subject are herewith revoked. With certain qualifications. It is agreed at the administrative level that you may continue temporarily in your position but your failure to detect the true purpose and meaning of "Doris Jensen" must yet be held against you. This was still your responsibility and you muffed it. Although you did a good job and showed much energy in retracing the steps and may have even gotten us out of it a little bit ahead.

The fully documented nature of your report is appreciated and will be forwarded to the FCC for desired action in this case. Penalties appear likely and I think that we can all feel happy about that.

At the same time, the objections to recent participants continue and I must advise you that unless some change in this area is shown immediately, the situation will have to be reviewed. You may, then, consider your status "probationary" although "probation" is a weak term for your actual position at this time.

Marvin Martin is not pleased. He has asked me to tell you this in exactly that way: that he is not pleased. Recent participants have not even been minimally acceptable. There has been some breakdown in the division for which you are responsible and it is harder and harder, he advises, to put a decent presentation together. Network is not pleased; he is not pleased. What do you plan to do about this? Please prepare plans, documentation, program of action, remedies, etc., for delivery tomorrow morning, three copies double-spaced.

Marvin Martin wishes me to advise you that he feels we are approaching a crisis-situation shortly and must do everything within our power, given fair warning, to protect against this.

XV

COPE: So there I was. You understand what I'm saying to you? Two hundred and eighty thousand dollars right in my hand.

MARTIN: Extraordinary. How many of us have ever had our heart's desire so close to touch?

COPE: Two hundred and eighty thousand. The horse run in at six to five as I explained to you so that means that the hundred twenty-five I come to bet with turns into two hundred and eighty. It's mathematical. I'm standing there outside the hundred-dollar cashier's window with that kind of money in my hand and I tell you as I was stuffing it away, the strangest feeling came over me. You wouldn't believe that feeling.

MARTIN: Try me.

COPE: You couldn't. No one outside of being there could understand.

MARTIN: You wanted that money, Cope. You wanted it very badly. And as it lay in your hand you began to get the feeling that it had become yours.

COPE: No. No, Mr. Martin, it was not like that at all, not the least bit.

MARTIN: It would be better if you called me Marvin. Consider us friends having a genial talk before a fire. In the distance sounds of rumbling in the theatre but this means nothing; it is just the two of us. The fire crackles, the smoke forms plumes around. Call me Marvin.

COPE: All right. All right, Marvin, you're still wrong even on a first-name basis. Let me explain.

MARTIN: I'm not stopping you. You're a bit wordy, Cope.

COPE: Listen, I wanted it very bad. You bet your life I did, but I didn't think that I was really *entitled* to it. How could I think that? I was only the runner, you see, the guy carrying the bets to the track for a hundred a week plus tips. As I said. That couldn't entitle me to two hundred and eighty grand. It wasn't mine, it wasn't anybody's. It was just a lot of money like what's lying around in the bank, it doesn't even belong to the bank, it's there to be cut up if anyone entitled to it wants it. How could I think it was mine? I'm very positive about that part of it.

MARTIN: But we know you wanted it, Cope. That's clear. You wanted that dough. It was big green, it was the easy marker. Is that how you people refer to it? Big casino.

COPE: Big casino is cancer.

MARTIN: Just testing, Cope, just testing you. Go on.

COPE: Okay. All right, it was. That part of it is true; I wanted it something terrible.

MARTIN: Of course you did.

COPE: But the distinction I wanted to make is that I didn't believe I was *entitled* to it.

MARTIN: Small-minded, petty and stupid. That's what it feels like to live on the margin. Remember that. Let's put it into our case notes.

COPE: Here I was, then. Fifty years old at that time, you understand? A fifty-year-old messenger with a sick wife and a kid who hated me.

MARTIN: Perfectly comprehensible.

COPE: I had never gone anywhere. I never done nothing. I hadn't accomplished a thing with my life except being the guy who ran the bets for the boys and carried back the money if the layoff worked.

MARTIN: Who were the boys?

COPE: Oh well, you know. The guys. The guys who took the bets and all that.

MARTIN: You mean The Mob?

COPE: There's no such thing.

MARTIN: You were a Mob employee. You knew them so well you called them the boys?

COPE: No. That's not right. There ain't no such thing as the mob, you got to believe that, the mob is a fiction. It's just made up, there's no organization. Everything gets done in pieces.

MARTIN: Just speculating.

COPE: Anyway, here I am, standing there and all of a sudden it hit me. This is where I'm standing and this is where I'm going to be for the rest of my life unless I take this chance that I was given. Two hundred and eighty. Two hundred and eighty *grand*. I never even *thought* money like that; if I would dream a little I'd think of six hundred, seven hundred dollars picked up off the street. The biggest bundle I had ever seen before that was seventy and that time I had coverage at the track. There was a guy with me; they didn't trust me so good back in the old days.

MARTIN: They still had fear of you at the beginning. They trained you not to be a man.

COPE: Oh? Oh. Well, anyway. Anyway, this time the deal, whatever they were doing, who can tell, it works and they put this horse over at six to five so I go out there with one twenty five which is big enough and then I'm standing around with all that money. That money, you understand, and the terrible part of it is that they think so little of me that they know I can be trusted. They got me in such a hole that they know all I'll do with the two hundred and eighty is to run right back and lay it on them for a present, less twenty dollars and subway fare.

MARTIN: That was what they paid you. Twenty dollars a day?

COPE: Twenty a day and expenses. Sometimes I would get tips but not too often. A little something on Christmas and maybe once or twice during the year if I said the kid was having birthdays. He had a couple of birthdays a year. Now and then a drink, maybe.

MARTIN: Was it worth it? You thought it was, didn't you?

COPE: I don't know. I never thought about it; it was just a living. I never thought about it too much at all. I couldn't.

MARTIN: Thinking being your long suit, of course.

COPE: Huh? Oh. Anyway, I couldn't do it. I couldn't take that money back to them like that. It wasn't in me. I tried—

MARTIN: You're an awfully long-winded bastard, Cope, you know that?

COPE: What?

MARTIN: You go on and on but we hear nothing. Only the same things over and over again. Self-pitying rant goes only so far these days.

COPE: Well, that's easy for you to say. You can sit there and pick your shots. What am I supposed to do? You asked for my story, I'm laying it on you. What are you, some kind of priest?

MARTIN: Maybe. A little. The confessional overlay is part of the picture.

COPE: What's that?

MARTIN: We haven't yet determined what we are, that's all.

COPE: Big deal. You jokers really impress me a lot, you know. I never dealt with guys like you before; you must be hot stuff.

MARTIN: Hostile?

COPE: I'm pissed off.

MARTIN: The thing is, you never *wanted* that money. Never, not at all. That wasn't the thing on your mind; it was something else.

COPE: Sure I wanted it. Sure I wanted the money. I took it, didn't I? And took right off to Schroon Lake in the Adirondack Mountains. You're making me get ahead of the story.

MARTIN: Patience. We're starting to get somewhere now. I sense a revelation.

COPE: I ain't finished.

MARTIN: The revelation is coming. You were trying to prove to yourself that the money meant something to you. In actuality you had no use for it at all. You don't even understand money.

COPE: (Inaudible.)

MARTIN: You're a beaten, frightened, disgusting little man. You are of absolutely no consequence and it is impossible to take someone like you seriously. Here we see the face of the enemy and what we have found is that it is No Face. The only person who ever took you seriously was you and you see what happened then. Disaster, total disaster! There is nothing to fear here, as you can see. You should have learned to laugh at yourself like the rest of them and then you wouldn't have wound up grubbing pennies for your miserable little rented confessions.

COPE: (Indistinguishable.)

MARTIN: At least that's the beginning of it. There is more to say. But the essential futility of the archetype should be demonstrated here. I'm getting bored with this.

COPE: Now, listen—

MARTIN: I've listened very patiently to you, Cope. You have no complaints.

COPE: But look. Look! You had me here, didn't you? I came here to tell my story, isn't that the truth? You wanted to hear my story and when I tell it—

MARTIN: Marginal types. Always on the margin, the very rim of possibilities. Further and further we seem to get from the central material here. It's too easy. The challenge is gone. I'm getting restless.

COPE: Go—

MARTIN: I'm losing interest. It's almost all gone. Harder and harder it becomes to connect. I don't even know who you are, didn't even read the vitae sheet; I can do this stuff in my sleep now. Lies and rationalization, easy evasions, paper-thin, cut through them with a dull knife. No more fables, Cope. Whatever your name is. Pay attention now. What did the money really mean to you? Let's get to the heart of it and quit.

COPE: Stop it.

MARTIN: The thing is, you'd been impotent for twenty-seven years when all this happened or was it supposed to be twenty-eight? It's so hard to remember the details of these closet-tragedies; they slip away from one.

COPE: Look here, mister.

MARTIN: You're out of your league, Cope! Let me work; I can do it in my sleep. The money became a symbol of potency for you; you thought in your twisted little mind that you could recover your balls, that by seizing the green, you could seize yourself. Pitiful, mindless little equations. How could it work? How could you have believed it? The only crutch that would work for you would be a crutch, pure and simple. You haven't the elegance or complexity for metaphor.

COPE: I don't understand what you're saying but I want to say this: I don't like your attitude. I heard all about you but I didn't believe it; I figured this man only wants to give people a chance to speak out, take him on his own terms and don't make no false impressions. I came here with an open mind, that's what I did. But you been acting like a real son of a bitch.

MARTIN: No obscenities.

COPE: You been cursing.

MARTIN: It's my program. And you've fucked the whole thing up, Cope.

COPE: It ain't fair. It ain't fair. There's something wrong with the whole thing, this kind of business shouldn't be allowed.

MARTIN: Stop the taping. Stop the taping! Damn it, I don't want to go through this any more. Really, is this the best you can lay on me? You expect me to take this idiot seriously? Fishing in a barrel, that's all it is. There's no challenge. It's boring. Boring! Now you listen to me, you bastards, things are going to change here or you're all going to swing. Get this now: I want some fresh meat. I want some meaning. I want some excitement like in the old days. If you can't get me something worthwhile, well then, goddamn it, I'll go out and get it myself and if it ever comes to that point, well then—

COPE: Is that it? Can I get out of here right now or am I supposed to stay?

MARTIN: You—

XVI

Dear Mr. Hurwitz:

I was able to dig up your name as head of Participant Selection from an old agency catalogue and hope that you will not object to this direct form of address. More importantly, I have the feeling for the first time that I am now addressing a human being rather than an agency and it is far easier to appeal to a *Hurwitz* (who may, for all I know, be a machine) than that fat, multiple set of ghosts which I have always envisioned as *gentlemen*. But in not addressing you any more, gentlemen, in bidding you goodbye, I wish you no offense and hope that you will find some ladies.

Mr. Hurwitz. Some eight weeks ago I wrote to you in some detail about my background (I should say that I wrote to *gentlemen* but I hear rumors that *gentlemen* are allowed to shuffle into your office once a week to deliver summations and reports; there is some contact) with a request to appear for further interviewing for the *Revelations* show starring Marvin Martin. (I now understand how to make italics; you underline on the typewriter. I am always trying to learn something new; I have so much dead time to atone, little by little I pick up stray wisps and oddments of facts or procedure. Italics are either a way of denoting proper names in context or providing emphasis. I am trying to provide emphasis.)

I do not know whether you ever actually read that letter or not but in the case that you haven't, I enclose a copy to fill you in from the beginning. It would be easy to blame the federal mail service for these difficulties but I do not believe that private failures can be indiscriminately blamed on institutions (the space agency will teach you this since it is an agency compounded of private failures) and therefore I am not blaming the mails; instead I point out that you are showing a stunning lack of courtesy in not, at least, giving me the favor of a reply. No matter how briefly stated that reply might be. Things are no easier for me than they are for any of you and I would think that on the human, the inter-personal, if not the corporate level, there would be some possibility of communication here.

I envision you as a kindly man with twinkling eyes, Mr. Hurwitz; you look something like an aged light colonel or maybe a staff sergeant, there are wrinkles around your eyes which could be compounded from humor or fatigue but within those eyes sits a kindly light beaming and dazzling by turns of those eyes (I am obsessed nowadays by the sub-ject of *eyes*) which have seen everything take in more yet and register the spectacle of their disenchantment.

XVII

Under the new policies and procedures, I am forwarding this correspondence. Unless you feel otherwise, I will inau-gurate screening procedure. Do you approve?

XVIII

Returned. Don't get snotty, Hurwitz.

XIX

I'm not getting snotty; I'm trying to follow your own pro-cedures which now demand that I obtain clearance for screening. Do you want me to go ahead or not? No matter what he turns out to be, I think that this is a new item. We haven't dealt with many like this.

XX

Well, then, I don't see much here at all. The documents have been reviewed closely and do not seem to yield much in the way of a distinct personality or an idiosyncratic core. Anyway, why are you asking me this? Screening is not my affair. You're on thin ice, Hurwitz, and if you think that this is the way to a sense of humor you are incorrect. Do what you wish but *expedite*; there is a show to get on.

XXI

Dear Mr. Monaghan:

Thank you for your recent letter and for your ensuing let-ters of inquiry. Unavoidable delays in answering correspon-dence, due to our very tight and busy production schedule, mean that replies are necessarily delayed although we do respond to all correspondence addressed to *Revelations*.

We would be interested in seeing you for a preliminary interview at the above address, suite 204, on the first of the upcoming month. We suggest that you bring all materials relevant to your background in corroboration and any other items which you feel would be of interest in establishing you as a possible subject for *Revelations*.

At that time, a member of our screening staff will go through your materials carefully. We advise you in advance that due to the high proportion of applicants to eventual participants, you can hear from us only by mail after the interview and that no explanations can be offered in the event of refusal nor can we get into prolonged correspondence with you.

With all good wishes.

XXII

No one knew what to do with him, so eventually he was passed all the way up the line to me. This is proper. This is justified. In the last analysis I must take the responsibility although I am possessed of a staff which has only my doom at heart. They know exactly what has happened. They know the shape and substance of the Hurwitz disaster no less than do I. Now the chain of command seems to be a rope down which Hurwitz slides uncontrollably. They put him in my office on a Tuesday afternoon. Late Tuesday waves of pain and corruption seemed to come from his face, moving across and out of him like small explosions. His hands clenched and unclenched; he was occupied with a small piece of paper which he was, invisibly, trying to tear to shreds. I know the habit. A small man: five feet seven or eight perhaps, diminutive features, delicate limbs, the extraordinary fineness of those nervous hands disconcerting to Hurwitz who maintains certain stereotypes. "Well," he said, with what I can only have taken to be a nervous giggle, "well then, here I am."

"Here you are," I said. In front of me, neat in a blank-faced folder, sat the digest of his entrance interview, questionnaire, secondary interview, impressions of the interviewing panel and so on. "You've been a long time getting here too."

"Does this mean?" he said, giving the paper a final thrust and putting it somewhere underneath the desk, hopefully in a pocket, possibly on the floor, "does this mean that I'm going to be on the program, then? The thing is that I need to be on the program."

"You don't understand, Monaghan," I said, "they bumped you up to me because they can't make a decision. No one can figure out what to do with you; that's the only reason I got the case. You haven't told us anything."

"I've told you everything you wanted to know. I wrote you three letters, I filled out all the stuff on the question-naire, I had two interviews—"

"No," I said, "no. The letters were fine; they told us something about you. That's what we want to know, we want to get a line on a participant and you did good there. But the rest of it: the interviews, the discussion . . . nothing. You've told us nothing. I don't think that you're the kind of con-testant that we'd want on *Revelations*. If we don't know who you are, we can't show others who *they* are. It's a program policy to be fully briefed."

He leaned back on the chair, showed me his hands now empty of paper, tilted a look at the ceiling—wink at the win-dow, shake of his head—and then leaned closer. Hurwitz could feel the steamy breath of the ex-astronaut assaulting the pallor of his face; Hurwitz could feel, as if from a great distance, the tension level increase, the dimensions of the room tighten. Hurwitz is an anxiety neurotic, knows all of his moves from way back, nevertheless some hint of dis-placement, some foreclosure in circumstances, thrust me back toward him, confronting him face to face, and I said with a kind of horrid intimacy forced from the conjoinment, "You're holding back on us, Monaghan. You're not telling a thing; your letter promised all kinds of stuff but you really haven't given us anything that we can use. This isn't the kind of program you seem to think it is; we need hard facts, details."

"Listen," Monaghan said; there we were, nose to nose, only inches apart and an idiot impulse overtook Hurwitz: what would happen, he wondered, if he leapt forward and planted a fervent kiss upon the lips of the twenty-ninth man to land upon the Moon? The face of the twenty-ninth man to land upon the Moon was not unattractive; in certain circumstances its weary, bleached aspect could be perceived coming over comfortingly upon a thousand television sets strung through all the public places of the city; perhaps Hurwitz could declare himself, once and for all, over the line and find against the sealing lips of the astronaut a peace more profound than any he had known before. "Listen," Monaghan said again, "I was holding back on them. I wanted to see someone at the very top. Look here: I know how these things work. It's all policies, procedures, levels of approval. Just like at the agency. It's a massive institution. I wanted to hold back until I got into the offices of the man responsible; then I could lay the truth on him. You believe me, don't you? I mean, you don't think that I'd go this far, go all the way up to the line to lie, would you? Or would you?"

I don't understand, I wanted to say to him. I don't understand who you are and what you're doing; now this is not exceptional, all of his life, or at least for all of his seeming life people who he does not understand have been Hurwitz's sole occupancy; he has been dealing in total irrationality, dealing with people whose motives seem to be only a parody of motivation so this should not disturb him but at the present moment it does, it does very much indeed because Hurwitz, sad to say, feels that he is now approaching the end of the line. The signs have been there for a long time, now closure is the order of the day; Hurwitz feels himself being narrowed to a progressively smaller space, the firmament is closing down on him, now he scrabbles on walls that seem to be at arm's length. But I said none of this to him, of course, Hurwitz being a totally rational man. Rationality poured from the Hurwitz air conditioners, sanity from his solid oaken desk, balance and equilibrium from the two-hundred-dollar manufactured but very well-fitting shirt in which he took his informal ease. So that all that I said was, "Your statements seem to conflict. At certain points in the questionnaire and interviews you seem to be saying that the agency is a total fraud, that none of these flights were ever conducted, that the program was a studio job but then, later on, in other interviews, you talk about astronauts having gone mad in orbit, astronauts having gone crazy on the moon or in one of the stations and having to have been forcibly restrained, prison camps for astronauts in which they were kept between missions so that they could not reach the outside world, rehabilitation centers for astronauts so that they could be cured of their insanity before being released and so on. It's not consistent. There is no consistency here whatsoever. It does not look to me as if you are clear on any of the facts or details here."

"You don't understand," he said hoarsely, leaning further forward, leaning back, moving sidewise, describing a small perimeter around and about before me, tapping his hands under the desk, a perfect neurasthenic case with whom in different circumstances Hurwitz could have communed deeply, "I did all of that deliberately to test your sincerity.

To find out if you were really listening to what I said, if what I was mattered at all or if I would only be used. When I came to the very top man I figured that I could tell the truth. If I could get to the top man. Which I did. You're the head; I know that. I researched you already and everything like that. You control the whole show, Mr. Hurwitz; the other is just a front."

"You should only know."

"I don't have to know. All that I have to do is have the right instincts. I have those instincts; I got them the hard way; a certain sense. Now we can talk."

"There's no consistency. A participant in the *Revelations* format has to be consistent; otherwise there's no way to make it work. You can't say one thing, then say another."

"We're both the same," Monaghan said and reached out, grabbed a Hurwitz pinky, twisted it, sending small waves of pain through the Hurwitz tendrils; pain which was refracted into the consciousness only as corruption, how far has Hurwitz fallen. "I've been waiting four weeks to finally face you, man to man across a desk. All the way through I knew that if I could only get to you we could reach understanding. I have waited for this moment, worked toward it. Now at last I can make someone understand."

"On April fourth you told an interviewer: 'We have never gone to the moon. We have never gone beyond brief journeys into the stratosphere and the planting of unmanned satellites in orbit. Everything else was contrived by the government to appear as if we had accomplished what we hadn't through the cunning use of the media and photographic techniques. Or maybe the government isn't to blame; maybe the decision was made at the agency level to lie and the government accepted this because it suited its purposes.'"

"Yes, I said that. I remember saying it."

"On April fifteenth you stated in a long questionnaire: 'Twelve of the sixty-eight men who have actually flown to the moon are now incurably insane. Three of them have attempted suicide, several others have made unprovoked assaults upon their wives or relatives. It is the very quality of the moon experience which has done this to them, a fact which the agency has kept from the public because if this fact had been known, the project would have collapsed in a fit of revulsion years and years before it did.'"

"I wrote that. I definitely wrote that."

"There's no consistency! They don't jibe."

"You said that already, Mr. Hurwitz. You said that I lacked consistency and I agreed. It was all a plan, don't you understand, a plan to get to you."

"I don't like it."

"And besides," Monaghan said hoarsely, "besides that, what does consistency matter? Why are you so concerned about consistency: don't you understand that nothing makes sense? I was a consistent man for three decades, I wanted everything to fit together, to make profound sense, I believed in ends and means, means and ends, a fusion of principles, cause and effect; I crucified myself on the scientific rationale and where did it get me? Look! Look where it got me! Try a little mysticism, Mr. Hurwitz; you won't be sorry. The pieces don't fit, they'll never fit the conventional way. You have to go outside of it."

"I want the truth," I said, leaning back on the chair, putting the Hurwitz legs on the desk, letting a little alley of perception move from his eyes to my groin, then upwards, hopefully, and out the line of the windows, "what we're in, all of us, is the truth-getting business. If you don't tell me the truth I have no time for you; if you want to continue the interview you'll have to give it to me."

"That's what I'm here to tell, Mr. Hurwitz, but you should understand by this time too that there's no such thing as objective truth; it's only a mystery, we've come to this point of time, to this stage of history because we've been taken here by men who believed in an objective truth, in a reasonable set of principles and look where we are! Madness, dislocation! There are subtleties—"

"No time," I said. "No time, no time; Hurwitz does not have the moments to listen to this any more. Are you an astronaut or a fool, a contestant or a ringer? Did we make flights to the moon or did we dream it all? Are there mad astronauts or is the agency itself demented?"

"You talk very well, Mr. Hurwitz. Somehow, I didn't expect you to talk this well."

"They have a place for it in the business," I said. "Now tell me, Monaghan, tell me what you have to say or be gone. Any way at all it makes no difference to me but time; time is the only quality that cannot be replaced."

"I'm impressed. I'm really impressed."

"Talk to me," I said. "I'm listening, finally."

XXIII

Hurwitz has a vision and in this vision he has never heard of *Revelations. Revelations* indeed does not exist; when a short guy named Martin Nickels came out of the midwest fifteen or twenty years ago he decided to go into the agency business rather than to stick with the media. Resultantly Martin Nickels is a very successful account executive today or perhaps busily working on a hitch in the Pilgrim State Hospital; he is not Marvin Martin, the famous cultured host of the Program of Humanity and no one named Hurwitz or ever named Hurwitz is the head of the procurement department, putting fresh meat on Marvin Martin's table every Tuesday at eight p.m., seven p.m. international time with all syndication and dramatic rights reserved to the proprietors.

Marvin Martin does not exist; *Revelations* does not exist: in this vision Hurwitz is a teacher. He is a professor of sociology and statistics at an eastern university or perhaps he is thinking of a boys' prep school, a prep school in the bucolic and pastoral section of southern New Jersey where under his gentle and only slightly homosexual hand boys are time and again eased into the slow passage toward manhood, Hurwitz's benign if somewhat obsessed gaze stamping itself indelibly into those recollections which they will entertain thirty or forty years hence when they are executives in the media. "If only I could have been like Professor Hurwitz," these executives will murmur in their darkest moments, "if only I hadn't wanted to make a buck; if only I hadn't been greedy and unaware of the things in life that are really important." They will come to that realization, Hurwitzian integrity will haunt them but in the meantime, holding against that day, they sit in his classes while he outlines for them large sociological movements, vast cultural tendencies. "You see," Hurwitz will tell them in his course *America as the Post-Industrialized Society: Post-Industrialization as Culture Lag*, "you see, inevitably what will have to happen in any post-technological society is that it will be dominated by machinery and institutions; the institutions will be as barbarian at the core as anything in the pagan role and eventually these institutions, through machinery, will gobble up everything, there will be nothing left on the landscape but gleaming edifices and a few staggering forms looking for an entryway, all of it dominated by the whir of machinery that somehow, ominously, does not quite work but as the culture becomes more hugely impersonal, as the barbaric and terrible machinery acts more and more concisely to squeeze all idiosyncrasy, all humanity, all individual voice out of the culture, as all of this is going on the institutions will out of necessity have to pay some lip-service to the tradition from which they emerged; culture lag is the factor here and the institutions will simulate flexibility, will simulate humanity, they will act through their devices in such a way as to assure the individuals trapped within them that they remain constant, remain human and the name of this will be public relations but all of this will be calculated as well, post-technologically speaking, to lower resistance to the take-over. The machines are taking us over, there is very little time left; perhaps there is no time at all because this was fated a long time ago but on the other hand there is just enough incompetence built into the technology to produce a peculiar kind of tension; this tension assures that the struggle will go on for a long time between those last elements on the fringes and the machinery itself. The machines and institutions are taking over, they have everything, but they are not quite sure about this, culture-lag having left them without an ethic quite suitable to their condition and this is what will make the society so interesting. No society which contains the possibility of imminent dissolution can ever be dull or without promise; that will be the case here for some time to come. Do you understand that, gentlemen? There will be a multiple-choice quiz on this tomorrow; thirty questions answer *a*, *b*, *c* or *d* and you will be expected to remain on the alert so keep your notes up to date and try not to let your minds or what you allow to pass for your minds wander too greatly. If that is all right. Class is dismissed for the day, gentlemen; I see that they are doing some further excavation on the quadrangle."

After his lectures Hurwitz will go home: he will live in a gentle faculty college not half a mile from the classrooms of this exclusive boys' boarding school; in the cottage his wife and children, all girls, will be there to greet him and the little girls, always inert after the first flashes of greeting will lie dark and quiet in their rooms while Hurwitz and his wife enjoy a mid-afternoon snack and coupling on the floor of their shielded patio. "I wanted to change lives," Hurwitz will say to his beautiful wife as he rams his genitals, now extended to their fullest, barely known capacity, by the lush thighs of his eager and submissive wife deep into her, feeling the answering thrill and response locked deep in her secret channels, "I wanted to change the way in which people regarded themselves. I wanted to affect the consciousness of those with whom I dealt; I wanted to help people to understand the nature of events occurring so that they could make some pattern and order out of them and in that way be able to protect themselves. Oh God," Hurwitz will groan, immersing himself in his wife's gigantic breasts, feeling the nipples churn like transistors under his touch, "oh God, I thought that you could do it with anyone, adults even, but came late to the realization that the only salvation was with the young, that if they had not been utterly corrupted by the age of sixteen then they were idiots but maybe you could catch them early, plant a little seed," and with that Hurwitz plants a little seed himself, springing with a grunt deep into the mysteries of his wife who thrusts back but never speaks, never says anything to him, responds to him only with a yielding softness and silence that goeth beyond peace, "but now I even wonder about that," he will add, rolling off his wife and looking at the roof of the patio, the trembling vines, the drooping plants, the greenery to the right and left of him, crocii and birds prowling in the garden: a perfect Utopian vision for Hurwitz, a perfect approximation of his goals and life and Martin Nickels a hundred miles to the north aggrandizing himself quietly, *Revelations* not even a glimmer, network not even a belief, ratings not even a hoax while deep in the bosom of his gentle wife Hurwitz nurses and suckles himself to sleep, shuddering into and past a long nightmare in which he has become the procurement chief for a complex and dangerous television program which deals with the destruction of participants for the entertainment of the greater army of the destroyed without. Hurwitz emerges shrieking but quickly recumbent in his wife's arms: the birds hop; the crocii bloom, he resolves that he will think no more of this. Impossible alternatives, no matter how dreadful, are always impossible he reminds himself. He can still change people's lives. He can still alter irrevocably the way in which people regard themselves. He still has a chance; he was not greedy, he was not aggrandizing, he did not lock himself into a mad trap but took his master's degree and opted for the clean, sweet serenity of the countryside.

XXIV

I have now had a chance to interview Walter Monaghan and recommend that he be utilized as a participant on *Revelations*. See full report and details attached. There is no question that he will be an unusual and rewarding guest and in coming to terms with the format of the program should yield some insights of the most profound nature.

I am available for consultation on this if necessary but feel that I have nothing to add to the full report and trust that further arrangements can be made. As you are well aware, our recent difficulties have been very much uppermost in my mind and it is with the greatest sincerity that I say that in finding this contestant I believe that I have redeemed myself or at least have redeemed the program. I realize that this is out of my hands but suggest that Monaghan may be the first series-participant we may ever consider; there is more than enough here for two fascinating programs as you will see. Thank you very much for your attention; this is, you can be sure, most respectfully submitted.

XXV

SMITH: And it's all a question of acceptance.

MARTIN: Of course it is. Social approval. And all of this is relative. Nevertheless, the fact is that you're a pederast; isn't that the truth?

SMITH: I don't even know what that means.

MARTIN: The admission of homosexuality was easy; you weren't giving away anything, not in those days, it was almost a badge of honor. Certainly acceptance. And the society you organized was really middle-of-the-road; couldn't even be called libertarian. "Give us our rights." Your mere acknowledgment of your status as homosexuals indicated that you *had* your rights. But pederasty was something different, wasn't it? And that's what you really had in mind.

SMITH: I told you, I don't even know what that means.

MARTIN: You've got some intelligence, Smith, don't be coy with me! We know exactly what it means and so do our friends out there. That was what you had in mind all the time;

the development of a socially approved rationale, a front so to speak, for your *real* activities. Once you were a labeled, identifiable homosexual, a *leader* so to speak, in the battle for homosexual rights, once that had been developed—

SMITH: That all happened a long time ago. Homosexuality hasn't been a cause for years and years.

MARTIN: Don't you interrupt me. Don't you *ever* interrupt me. It is not your function or place to do that.

SMITH: I was only explaining—

MARTIN: Your interest in young boys is fully documented as early as 1963. There is clear evidence on the record to show that at that time you deliberately seduced—

SMITH: Stop it. Please stop it.

MARTIN: We are investigating. We are in the process of narrowing a truth. Do not interrupt me again.

SMITH: But this isn't fair to me.

MARTIN: Boy-lover! Quiet! Let me continue.

SMITH: I never understood why people on your show begged for mercy. It was never clear to me how anyone who volunteered for this in the first place would have any inclination or right to ask you to stop. I was hasty, intolerant; I acknowledge my weakness. I cannot take this any more.

MARTIN: You're not going anywhere, Smith. Sit tight. As a matter of fact your name is not Smith; it is Kulski, Harold Kulski and I am no longer willing to accept your pseudonymity since you are unwilling to cooperate. No one wants to cooperate any more. Your name is Harold Kulski and you are twenty-eight years old; you are employed in the third Federal division of supply and ordnance for the fifth western region and your residence is presently at—

SMITH: Stop! You have no right!

MARTIN: I can do anything I want. Anything that I want to do is permitted. Don't you go around delineating people's rights, Kulski! This is *Revelations* and here at last the mystery is made flesh, the lies fall away from us as the driven snow and we confront the naked, raving face of the truth. Nothing can be interposed before the truth, do you dig that? The truth is sacred: it is high, it is deadly, it is concealed and it is often uglier than darkness . . . but it is the highest crown to which we can aspire and *nothing* blocks it. Go on, cry: break open, run like blood. By the way, there's no exit from the set until we release you. Pederast! Boy fucker! For God's sake, will someone get me something *worth* this passion?

XXVI

Cold, malicious April evening; roiling clouds to the west, rain falling like blood. I return to the west nineties to see "Doris Jensen" again. I prefer to call her "Doris Jensen"; this is the name under which I came to know her and she will always be "Doris" to me although this, of course, is not her name and never will be. I will not reveal her name. Her name is to remain private with me. These notes are not public, cannot possibly be made public, are squirreled like dead cockroaches into the bottom of Hurwitz's desk after he commits the unspeakable midnight act of writing them; nevertheless certain amenities must be observed. Even the journal must cultivate a certain dignity, a certain perspective: besides, and he will admit this, Hurwitz lives in the mad gleam of hope that after his death or disaster his possessions may be exhumed, these notes may be found, and even against his posthumous will they may be published as the finest and most concise statement of where the final quarter of the American twentieth century dwelt. Hurwitz is a fine writer; he has skills and devices, he can write simultaneously in the third and first person and make both equally mad, almost indistinguishable; Hurwitz has a gift for slashing characterization, keen compression; is it impossible for him to feel that his notes may someday be valuable? Once, a long time ago I wanted to write a novel called *Revelations*. It would have been about the quality of my life. Of course I have outgrown that.

Revelations. Doris Jensen. Last night I went to see her; we have become friends or at least reconciled enemies, also she throws at Hurwitz a rowdy good fuck of a dimension and eagerness he has not encountered in many years. The tolerance level of Hurwitz is a straight curve upward; now he needs larger and larger jolts of perversity to establish the connections which he made so simply in his naive teens, his hopeful twenties. In addition to her abilities in bed (opening Hurwitz up to a corruption and need which he thought had been drained long out of him) Doris is a splendid conversationalist; she and Hurwitz discuss all of the topics of the day, subjects of the night, the agreement being that specifics of her own job will never be questioned and Hurwitz will not ask her, ever, how she is progressing. On the other hand, Hurwitz will tell her everything she needs to know of him, feeling that he has nothing left to protect.

"I tell you everything," I say to her on the west side of Manhattan, "I keep no secrets from you, professionally at any rate. This is extremely dangerous. How do I know that you are not conveying anything backwards?"

"Then why talk to me that way?"

"Because I need you," I say, "I need you, I need to be heard. I do not care." A breast bobbles within perspective, I seize it with trembling hands, cup it, knead it, drink my fill trying to think only blank thoughts and pass with Doris into a long, dry, tumbling emptiness; somewhere in the center of it she grips me and urges me to go higher, harder, faster, deeper, I probe into her and feel the slackness of her flesh, all tension crumbling, move toward the center, feel my orgasm come only as an unnecessary appendage to the need to bring her own sensations, press, squeeze, perform the unspeakable under and around her and she collapses around me groaning, I feel myself being devoured by her flesh, sinking deep into its core, sweet and sour smells coming off from her, everything damp and we fall apart like dancers. "I need you," I say uninterruptedly, "and know that this is so. You listen. You say nothing. I can tell you everything; I have no conception of what you are thinking and to what consequences. I find this titillating, even exciting." She rolls away from me, looking for a cigarette. "Isn't that so?"

"You don't even know who I am," she says. "You're just taking it on faith."

"Do you want me to know? Do you want to establish a deeper and more meaningful relationship?"

"No," she says, "God forbid, no," and lights the cigarette, tosses the match away from her with a whisk to the side of the room, lies flat on her back, breasts sliding apart from one another and exhales. "No more. No more meaningful relationships. Never again."

"That man will destroy the program," I say. "I am convinced of it. If he actually gets on the tape he will be the end of *Revelations*. Nevertheless, I am obsessed by him."

"What man?"

"Monaghan."

"Oh yes, Monaghan. Why are you obsessed by him?"

"This is very private. I am not sure that I can lay a finger on it, even a pinky. Let me say that he interests me."

"Why will he destroy the program?"

"This I do not care to discuss."

"There are many things that you don't care to discuss this evening."

"I want to get laid," I say. "I want to get laid profoundly. I want to have sex so devouring that it will be the obliteration of consciousness." I put a finger on a nipple, tweak it, feel the slight rising, withdraw and let the finger trail down the lines of her stomach. Small white lines of depression are left by this finger; her flesh sags; lacking resiliency, it carries the pressure marks for some time. Looking at this flesh it is impossible to believe that it is capable of being the receptacle of such sensations. I pinch it, see the blood rise, move my hands below her waist.

"No," she says, pushing me away. "That won't work. We've already done that. I can't do it twice."

"Try," I say. "Try."

"I thought you wanted to talk."

"I thought I wanted to talk too but I was wrong. I don't. I merely want to commit, to conjoin, to engage. Do you understand what I'm saying?"

"You're talking about fucking."

"Exactly."

"I thought you were talking about fucking but I wasn't sure. I know all about that."

"He interests me," I say, turning, poising, putting a finger on the cigarette and lifting it with her to the ashtray to extinguish it in a small foul whiff of odor, reminiscent of the thigh or palm. I mount her. "He interests me very much. You could not understand how he interests me," and feel my restored genitals poking and prying at her again. Amazing, amazing: not two months ago Hurwitz complained of psychic impotence, now bear him witness. Observe how he pumps, observe how he moves, observe how his extended equipment moves in hush and mystery toward its secret object. Hurwitz groans, he shudders, his teeth are bared, his body convulses. His mustaches twitch. Now he feels an onslaught more venomous than any he has yet known; substance like acid rising within him. "I'll fix him!" Hurwitz cries and moves into the last agonies, "I tell you, I'll fix him! I'll fix him for this, he can't do it to me any more." Orgasm comes over him like a shroud; he does not cease speaking but he ceases to hear himself speak. He moves into a small, small cavern and for that evening is heard from no more. Much later, in a daze, images of Monaghan occur to him but satiated he does not react; what drove him toward Monaghan is for the moment quiescent and he sleeps. Hurwitz sleeps deeply. For the rest of the evening he thinks no more. He is at peace.

Midnight comes. He leaves.

XXVII

It may all be a plot. This possibility has occurred to Hurwitz several times; he is not entirely stupid. "Monaghan" may be as much a creation as "Doris Jensen"; "Monaghan" may be a last arrogant attempt to destroy *Revelations* through the induction of yet another dangerous participant. It is doubtful that they would be so stupid as to risk another attempt after Hurwitz so cleverly saw their recent ploy . . . but then it would have been equally doubtful that Hurwitz, after all his struggles, would have become sexually and emotionally linked with "Doris Jensen." Who would have guessed that after his explosion of insight, his surehanded and destructive manipulation of the woman, he would have begun with her a covert relationship? This was surely not predictable. By the same token another effort to destroy Hurwitz and his program on the heels of the earlier one may have the advantage of surprise.

What do I know of "Monaghan"? There does indeed exist a file on a man of this name but how do I know that he is not dead or mad and this one merely an assumption of his identity? Have I checked this out? Is it possible in any case to verify something like this?

Questions: questions. Hurwitz is battered by such questions! Such doubt and indecision infest his rather bulky frame that it is sometimes speculative how he ever gets anything done. Nevertheless he is a responsible man; he is surehanded, he has purposes. What does Hurwitz know of astronautics? Look it up in a book. What does he know of the space program? Seek advice from an expert. What does he know of "Monaghan"?

Ask Doris Jensen.

XXVIII

Dear Mr. Hurwitz:

Rolling into the first orbit of the moon, looking at it come up against us, harsh and flat, unyielding and deadly, I could feel the panic coming over me: could sense the panic in the others as well. "We cannot do this," I wanted to say to them, "cable back to the base and tell them to forget the whole thing. We are not meant to walk on surfaces this savage, we are not meant for this coldness and furthermore the weightlessness is making me absolutely sick to say nothing of the instructions, the constant instructions they keep on sending us from the Base: don't they give us any credit whatsoever for independent thought and action? Are we to be totally run by machines? Have the machines taken over everything? Tell them to forget it; tell them that we will not perform the mission, tell them that it was all a lie and mistake and that we will remain in orbit until the impulses

from control are fed into the computers permitting us to
return. Tell them that we cannot take any more of this, that
we will not be machines and that from the bowels of our
humanity we deny willingness to walk upon the moon. Tell
them that right away; I'm not the communications man or
I would," I wanted to say to them and looking into their
cold, dead faces, as spiritless and beaten as my own, sensed
that they wanted to say the same to me but the training
was effective, the training had worked very well, the training was definitely the very best that a grateful government
could afford and thus no speeches of that type were passed
among the crew on that mission. "Check the g-rate," we
said to one another, and "better verify the cannisters" and
"that apogee looks a little bit off; better ask for a computer
check" and so on and so forth, the comments crackling as if
we were wearing several layers of steel in that craft and not
our underwear (we always did most of our traveling in our
underwear, weightlessness is easier to accommodate in that
fashion and embarrassing biological accidents more easily
contended) and in due course two of us, myself being one
of them, went down to the moon in a small craft and landed
and danced among some rocks, picked up some samples,
planted seismometers, engaged in geological verifications,
conducted a guided tour of a crater, told dirty jokes off the
transmission to one another and then returned to the ship.
In the ship, on the way back, the moon receding from view
was no less deadly than on the voyage in but now there
was nothing to say, even privately. The bags containing
samples, foul with little bulges, were tucked away in pock-
ets of the capsule, our suits were stowed in lockers, only
the bodies were left but this part of the equipment no less
than any of the others seemed to sag with Mission Accomplished; a certain lack of energy might have been observed

in our motions and jokes to the Base were less frequent and entirely without humor. More than anything else, we were machinery that had been spent but this was something that I only came to realize later and in no context which was then useful. I was impotent for six months after returning from the moon; every time I hovered over my dear wife (my decontaminated frame lumbering, striving only to please) I had an image of rock, devastation and rubble; that image coming over me with such power and conviction that it was barely possible to guide my organ home and when I did so only to the most puerile and embarrassing result. "It's all right," she would tell me time and again, "it's all right; we have all the time in the world, now just be patient," and then after so many months of that and finally squeezed out a small return she up and left me. What do you think of that? Sorry ladies; sorry gents, there is very little to be made of the situation.

This is an example of the many personal memories I have from my seven-year experience as an employee of the space-agency, the kind of memories which you suggested that I try to write down and send to you to give you further background for the *Revelations* program and help you persuade them to have me on the air. I have many other memories which I could also write you but I wanted to make sure that this was the kind of thing expected before I continued. I have saved up intimate personal journals for the past several months which contain, as best as I can recall, all of my more significant experiences while with the agency and I will resort to them again and again if only given the go-ahead by you.

At the same time I want to remind you that I am perishing here, literally perishing: there is absolutely no income in the first place and in the second I cannot stall off my creditors indefinitely by stating that I have a very good chance to appear on a national television program. Something must break soon; I suffer from depression, suffer from cold sweats so aching and close to the bone that I worry about gravitational stress, suffer from attacks of anxiety so profound and gloomy that I sometimes think I can encapsulate all of my fate in the smallest and most indecent of human acts, say rape or suicide. This cannot be permitted to continue; I deserve something too. Although I find as much irony in saying this as you must in reading it, I do remind you that I am a man who has spent many years in the service of the nation, your nation, Mr. Hurwitz, the nation of Marvin Martin (make of it what you will; it is still very much our land) and I am entitled to some consideration. Things cannot go on like this forever (or at least these are the words that I uttered to myself over and over again for comfort while on the way to the moon; how wrong I was) and there must be a point of stabilization or balance. I cannot be strung out indefinitely. Please advise me, thus, of your plans to have me as a participant on *Revelations* and advise me as well if this is the kind of recollection you are seeking and whether I should send you more.

XXIX

There is a fine, fierce implacability to their faces; a kind of bare, bleak removal of all sensation, even chronology, so that all that remains is the eyes, staring coldly out of that landscape, a strange, rising light to them, dead pallor to the cheeks, the hands, arms and gestures quiet and contained. He came in to see me without appointment at ten. One moment he was not there and the next he was, the secretary babbling behind him. "I *told* him he couldn't come in," she said, and "I didn't *allow* this," and in the one brief glance which the man and I exchanged I saw that we were brothers and sent the foolish girl out. She is without capacity; she believes in Marvin Martin. All of the subordinates here are hired by Martin himself; it is impossible for us to place any of our own people here. The man who had come in uninvited sat before me and opened a briefcase, looked over some concealed documents with an air of satisfaction and then closed the briefcase forever, put it under his feet. "Do you want to see some identification?" he asked. "Is that necessary?"

"No," I said. "I know who you are and where you're from. I believe that you are what you are."

"My name is John Mills. I am employed by the central security agency."

"I know that," I said. "I could see it. You don't have to tell me."

"You are considering for participation in your program a man named Walter Monaghan, an ex-employee of the space agency. Is that correct?"

"He's been interviewed. No final decision has been made on him yet."

"This man is unstable, highly disturbed, and to give him credence would menace the national security. I am here to advise you of this and to ask you what your plans are."

"I have no plans," I said and put my feet on the desk, looked at the immaculate, slightly linted Hurwitz socks, cast an eye toward the ceiling, neck toward the floor. "I merely work here. I go from day to day."

"As a citizen it is your responsibility to be advised of risk, of the nature of certain people with whom you are dealing."

"Are you telling me that we can't use Monaghan on the program?"

"Why would you want to use him?" Mills said, bringing his fingers against one another, looking up at the ceiling as if checking it for concealed weaponry. "Surely this advisement would be sufficient. You have the security of the country no less at heart than I do, Mr. Hurwitz. We know your record; we know your service. You won't want to disappoint us."

"It's not my responsibility," I said. "I merely screen applicants. The final decision is made by the upper echelons. I have very little leverage."

"That's true; we're quite aware of your responsibilities as they have been delineated. On the other hand, only those applicants who are approved by you ever get to these so-called upper echelons, so that's very simple right there."

"I've already approved him," I said. "I think that he would make a very interesting participant. Of course the man is totally insane, I see that. But insanity is titillating."

"You can disapprove him."

"The memo is in the works. I don't think you really understand how things work here; you can't rescind what you've already done. As I said, I agree that Monaghan is totally insane. I don't think it's necessary for anyone to take him seriously in order to see his merits as a participant."

"I don't think you know anything about Monaghan at all," Mills said, running his hands affectionately over the briefcase, tugging at the zipper, then replacing it, looking over my shoulder. "We've been into this case very deeply. We're very interested in this man, very interested."

"If you're so interested, why is he in the condition he is?"

"I don't understand what you're saying."

"I said, if the government is so interested in Monaghan, why is he poor, lonely and collapsing in a furnished room. Is that how the government shows its interest?"

Mills shook his head, shrugged, let some silence pass between us while he considered certain plaques and memorabilia on the Hurwitz desk. "You're being difficult," he said. "I don't think that you understand how any of this works. I don't think you're aware of the situation at all and I'm disappointed in you."

"*I'm* interested in Monaghan. At least I've listened to him."

"We're aware of what Mr. Monaghan has to say."

"You don't sound like you've spent much time listening."

"I don't think that this is getting too far, Hurwitz. I don't like your attitude."

"That's perfectly all right," I said. "I don't like my attitude either. I don't like anything about the situation; not a single thing and I don't see why I should. I wash my hands of it, I've passed him on to higher levels."

"So pass him down again."

"It's not that simple."

"Everything is simple. You make things complex where they are not, Mr. Hurwitz."

"Do you have a file on me?"

"Pardon me?"

"I said, how is my dossier."

"You misunderstand the government," Mills said with a delicate gesture, shoving his briefcase deeply into his gut and bending over it slightly, much as if it had punched him. "The paranoia of Americans is extreme. You project every single fear, inadequacy, lapse of behavior upon a disembodied figure which you call the government. The government can no longer bear the brunt, Mr. Hurwitz. We have problems of our own; we can't deal with neurotic fantasies any more."

"That's pretty strong stuff."

"Nothing is strong. I happen to be very mild; I was selected for this assignment because I am a temperate man. I don't want to think of what other agents might do."

"The riots are just beginning," I said pointlessly. "Just beginning. Wait a few years and see what happens."

"They don't have the technology," Mills said with a little smile. "It's all balanced the wrong way. If it comes to confrontation, the technology is in one set of hands. Remember that."

"I think our interview is concluded."

"It's concluded when I say that it's over, Mr. Hurwitz. Not before then."

"Listen," I said, trying to affect a pose of ease, nonchalance, an old Hurwitzian indulgence, appear controlled, much as if he were a petitioner for *Revelations* and I about to turn him down (more and more I regard almost everyone I meet as an unsuccessful candidate for the program; this may be a delimitation of relationships and on the other hand I may be exactly correct), "you don't have to go to me. Put the screws on from up above. Go to the upper echelons."

"That's not procedure at this time."

"Make it procedure then. Why bother me? I'm the little guy down at the bottom of the pole. Talk to the others; they'll really jump. They're afraid of everything."

"We know what's going on."

"Of course you do. So take it to Marvin Martin."

"Do not tell us how to run our affairs, Mr. Hurwitz."

"You're telling me how to run mine."

"I don't like your attitude," Mills said, standing, a strange uneasy grin poised now on his face. For the first time the bleakness wavered; something crept in at the corners of his eyes, lay there for a moment and then went away again but left its marks in the center of the face, streaks lying down front and center. "Don't tell the government how to conduct its business. The government has conducted its business very well for two hundred years, which is a lot longer than people like you have been around."

"Or people like you."

"I figured on the record that you would be uncooperative but I was willing to try. I am finished now, Mr. Hurwitz. I hope that you will give our talk some thought."

"I have no thought," I said. "You came to the wrong party. I am merely a functionary, on the lower levels of what you might consider a huge institution. I have no prerogatives, no leverage, no real weight. This is not to say that I won't think about our talk. I'll give it a lot of thought but the thing is that it simply won't be very constructive."

It is possible that he said something in response to this then but it is equally possible that he did not. One moment he was there and the next he wasn't, having apparently used the door for egress although he might have used the window as easily or perhaps the Hurwitz pocket. There he is, deep in the Hurwitz pants pocket, miniaturized of course (for better security; there is absolutely no describing the technological advances the government has made), a tiny elf, peering with bright mad eyes at the goings on. At one end there is a small shaft of light, pure office fluorescence beaming into the Hurwitz lining. At the other, through a tiny hole perceptible only to Hurwitz and small coins which dribble through are the Hurwitz genitals themselves, dark swinging meat covered by material thin as lint, a pendulum to Hurwitz's purpose, stalking him through the rooms of his life.

XXX

At eleven in the morning on Wednesday the summons came. Hurwitz has seen Marvin Martin once in his life on what could be called the personal level; now it will be twice. Hurwitz escorted by a small, unwieldy man with hands like ball-bearings moves up levels, down levels, through steel and glass, into corridors and emerges in the anteroom of Marvin Martin's offices. "I can't talk to you at all," the man with ball-bearing hands says to Hurwitz. "It's nothing personal, but I just have nothing to communicate."

"That's all right."

"If I had something to say I'd say it but there just isn't. I don't know anything. I just run messages back and forth and every now and then go out for a cup of coffee. So I can't give you any personal stuff on The Man at all even if you begged me. I hardly know him."

"It's okay. I don't care about that."

"If I had any personal stuff to tell about him at all I really would, but I don't know a thing. All I am is a messenger, if you follow what I'm saying."

"That's all right. I don't need to know too much about him."

"You see," ball-bearings says, "a man in my position, people get the idea that I have an in or something and all the time, always, they're asking about Marvin Martin, what he's really like. No, we don't take this elevator, we take that one, the private one. They figure that since I'm doing errands for him I have, like, an intimate connection, that I can give details on his habits or so on. They don't understand that this is just a job and you got to detach yourself from almost any job to stay in shape. You know what I mean?"

"I know what you mean," Hurwitz says, dodging an elevator operator, a receptionist and a small covey of bright-eyed men who sweep past him in a corridor, chattering to themselves about policies and procedures. "I know exactly what you mean and it's perfectly all right."

"Like does he take his coffee black or what he thinks of the Asian plan. I can't tell you."

"Enough idiosyncrasy," Hurwitz says, rather obscurely, as they move into a reception room. "I cannot bear any more idiosyncrasy. Things must remain level and flat; there must be a fine tempering action to the world. Unquestionably this is necessary; there can only be so much tolerance for aberration and then one must call a halt."

"I don't understand you."

"I bet his clothes stink from all the repressed sweat," Hurwitz says and ball-bearings looks at him diffidently, ball-bearings raises his eyes to those of Hurwitz and a small sliver of communion passes between them, a communion which seems to diminish ball-bearings rather than otherwise, causing him to both dilate and contract, turn to ash as it were under the penetrating gaze of Hurwitz and mumbling something or other he disappears from the vicinity of the Hurwitz gaze and goes out of his life forever. He is replaced by a blonde secretary with murderous eyes who says that Marvin Martin is busy. "Because thanks to the way things have been going here he has to do all the work himself. He'll be a few minutes late on his appointment; you'll have to wait."

"He asked for me."

"I have nothing to do with that," the blonde says and looks down at the papers on her desk, does something to her fingers and with quick, deadly gestures puts them on the keys of a typewriter which gives off the uneven spatter of a series of hand grenades. Hurwitz is left to his own devices: he surveys the expressionless, unadorned walls of the reception room, surveys his hands, delicate and trembling only slightly from the emotional burdens to which Hurwitz has been subjected, surveys the creases in his pants and other accoutrements of his clothing which reflect a certain Tuesday shabbiness and as always at times like these seeks to blank his mind, perish all thought which has always been a problem anyway, so little profit having come to Hurwitz from thought that he regards it as an accessory like leather furnishings in a passenger car. "Maybe you'd better give me your name again," the secretary says, still typing. "I have to keep the list up to date."

"He knows my name. My name is very well known to Marvin Martin."

"This may well be but *I* don't know it. Do you want to spell it out?"

"I didn't request this appointment," Hurwitz points out, rising smoothly to the bait. "I'm here at his request. He wanted to see me."

"I have no way of knowing that," the secretary says. She does something with her breasts, twists them, moves them inside her dress, bringing to Hurwitz old images of pain and necessity. "Spell it out," she says.

Hurwitz seems to contract, move in upon himself in the chair and he spells out his name. He does so reluctantly, pausing for breath between each letter and somewhere in the middle makes a mistake which he instantly corrects as he breaks into fumes of hot and cold sweats. "I think I recognize it now," the secretary says. "I didn't before because you have a tendency to mumble but now I know exactly who you are."

"Can I go in then?"

"I don't know," she says, running her hands down her stomach, touching herself invisibly below desk level as a pleased contemplative smile overtakes her from this contact with her private parts. "Let me check." She opens up the intercom, says something quietly into it while she regards Hurwitz and then says, "it's all right. He's free. You can go in right now."

"Are you sure that's all right?"

"I have nothing to do with policies and procedures," she says. "All I have are my own responsibilities."

"I'm sick of idiosyncrasy," Hurwitz says, standing. His ankles feel somewhat shaky, likewise his knees. Why is he trembling? "Idiosyncrasy, eccentricity, individuation—will be the death of me. Why can't all the characters be flattened out as in a pulp novel? Why do they all have to establish themselves in such ways?"

"I don't know what you're talking about."

"Life should be a pulp novel," Hurwitz mumbles and walks through a door. He swiftly turns, walks out, he has moved into a closet mysteriously cluttered with old clothing, papers, valises, the dense odor of impacted flesh, closes the door while the secretary watches impassively and then tries another one which opens into a long, long hall. "I don't suppose," he says, "that you'd be interested in trying a personal relationship of some sort?"

"What's that?"

"You wouldn't want to get involved and try to know me better, would you? There is nothing sexual about this whatsoever. Hurwitz functions sexually only in marginal circumstances, so I am not presenting that kind of proposal to you at all. I thought that we could merely talk some time at your convenience."

"I'm sorry. I have nothing to do with that at all. I'm not involved with anyone."

"I should have understood that," Hurwitz says agreeably and closes the door, moves down the corridor. His last vision of the secretary is rigidity, immobility, she is poised at her desk, one vagrant hand once again dropping toward her genitals and he retains this image, it is a good one, it can only stand him in good stead because even in his youthful forties, Hurwitz still finds it hard to believe that women react sexually whatsoever, take anything from obligation from their private parts. He finds himself at the end of a corridor before a golden door which bears the name MARVIN MARTIN upon it in raised letters; he gestures his way through and sees Marvin Martin sitting behind a large desk, refracting the rays of a sunlamp through fingers spread across his face, looking down at some pieces of paper before him. "Come in, Hurwitz," Marvin Martin says in a noncommittal way. "I've been waiting for you. It's been a long time."

"I was here ten minutes ago. I was outside talking to your secretary."

"That's not my problem," Martin says and shuts off the sunlamp. He shakes his head when released from the glare as if reconstituting himself, pushes the papers to one side and leans back, his arms behind his head, chair tilted, looking at the ceiling. "A very long time," he says. "It's been several years since our last talk."

"I'm aware of that."

"It will probably be several years until our next. If I retain you," Marvin says. "Do you want to sit down or would you be more comfortable standing?"

"I think I'd be more comfortable standing."

"Me too," Martin says. He stands, turns, closes all the drapes behind him until the room seems to be bathed in a mild, red fluorescence coming from the walls, peers under his desk as if to check certain equipment, appears to turn a switch or two, stands. "There's no reason for you to be afraid of me."

"I didn't say I was."

"On the other hand, there's no reason why you shouldn't. You've made a lot of problems for us, Hurwitz, too many problems, and you've come to my attention rather closely. It's best if people don't come to my attention."

"Do you want to release me?" Hurwitz says. He has meant his voice to be firm, demanding, authoritative but instead it comes out like a dismal peep; the first bleat of a chick staggering out of a shell could not be more tentative and pained. "Do you want to release me?" he asks, trying again and the peep modulates somewhat, becomes more the expression of a full-grown hen or at least a potential one. "Because if you do, that's that."

"Not necessarily. People I release get released by memo. You're so fearful, Hurwitz: it's almost no use dealing with you. I got this feeling before, that you dwell in fear. You have absolutely no sense of options, which is a sad thing. No, I just wanted to talk to you a little. We will have a conversation and then you will go on your way. The government was in touch with me recently about one of your recommended participants. The government and I had a long talk about this participant, the program and you. I wanted to clear up certain things on that level."

"I don't know anything about it," I said rather sullenly. "I mean, they were in to talk to me and I referred them to you. That's all I know. He seemed to check out pretty good with me, Monaghan."

"Monaghan," Marvin Martin said. "At least I know that we're talking about the same individual, Walter Monaghan. You know, Hurwitz, you people misinterpret me wholly; I'm not looking for sycophancy. That isn't the kind of thing I want at all; this constant atmosphere of fear and dependency infuriates me. What I'm looking for is men who can stand up, make broad independent judgments, lay them straight on the line with me and say, 'Marvin Martin, if you don't like what I have to say, then why don't you just fuck yourself?' That's all I'm seeking. The other parts disgust me, they bore me; I haven't looked for that in a long time. Stop being so defensive!"

"I'm not being defensive."

"Yes you are, Hurwitz, and it's disgusting! Disgusting, do you understand me? We need men who can take positions and fight them through. Look at me. Do I look like the kind of man who feeds on dependency and fear?"

I looked at him. Forty, forty-five, maybe fifty, the slow sheen coming off his face, containment in his gestures, ease in his posture, looking very much the way he did on the media but better since the color was, so to speak, natural and the connection over the desk was immediate rather than filtered through. A short man, short like Monaghan, five feet seven or something but giving the impression of great height from a seated position, the legs short and unre- markable, the torso elongated and poised, a man built to sit, to regard, to compose and discuss, a cunning in the eyes which might be mistaken for alertness by an unwary con- testant. "No," I said. "No, you don't look that way to me."

"I called you in for a different reason, Hurwitz. I called you into this office to tell you that I've decided to go ahead. I like your participant. I like the way Monaghan looks. I'm going to take him and the government be damned. That's what I told the man and now I tell you. So don't buckle under if they come to you in the night."

"I'm delighted to hear that."

"I'm looking for something. No one understands that, no one understands that my purposes are serious, that I am not just passing through here, that there is something very basic that I need and I have been looking at it for a long time now but only from a great distance. This production is my life, do you know that, Hurwitz? I have everything tied up in *Revelations*. There isn't anything frivolous about this. My purposes are entirely serious and I am going to be taken seriously."

"All right," I said. I backed off from him slightly, the Hurwitz nose twitching slightly from an infusion of new orders; it occurred to Hurwitz that Marvin Martin might be drunk. This would be a stunning contrast from his last interview with Marvin Martin but that was seven years ago and as we know every cell in the human body is replaced within seven years. The new, slightly teetering Marvin Martin returns to his chair and says, "Everything in me is tied up in this program. It's my entire life. Maybe you begin to understand why I take everything so seriously."

"*Revelations* is my life too."

"No it isn't. Don't say that Hurwitz, don't even pretend to think it; *Revelations* is just a stopping point for you; you rest your cowardice and corruption here but it could as well be anywhere else, something otherwise to project your frustrations and fear on. It's nothing personal but with me, Marvin Martin, it is deeply personal. I love this program. It means everything. Do you know why?"

"I think so."

"I think not. I had a dream, Hurwitz; let me tell you about this dream and it was that Americans could finally confront themselves. All over this nation we have institutions, massive institutions, repressing humanity, driving everything down to mechanicalness and dread, the individual idiosyncratic act squeezed out forever and in this I saw the death of the country, but I had an idea. Marvin Martin had an idea: we must be brought once again to terms with ourselves because that is the only salvation, to see the palpating humanity underneath, to touch the naked nerve of connection. I carried that idea around for thirty years, saw it in the night, felt flashes of it in the day and this is what I worked. I was only an adolescent during the time of assassinations; a very young man, but I knew then that the game had been changed, there was an entirely new set of imperatives, something had to be done to restore us to ourselves before the whole thing was blotted out of existence by machinery and the engines of death. I could see it all coming, could smell it in the air, if we did not get to the human parts of ourselves soon there would be nothing left. I am called a cruel man but it is for love."

"I don't want to hear this," Hurwitz says. "This is none of my affair. I do not want your justifications or biography. It is all too late for that."

"From what part of yourself did you dig out that whine, Hurwitz? From where the protest?"

"You said you wanted no sycophancy. I tell you that I do not want to hear your justifications but I am glad that you are going to use Monaghan."

"You'd better watch your step, Hurwitz," Marvin Martin says, using a finger to ring the air, heaving in his chair, poising lightly over the desk in an attentive position and Hurwitz sees that he is not drunk at all, no liquor in his system, no pot in his bowels, it is all posture, gesture, Martin has controlled again. "We've had our eye on you for quite a while now and you're already on your way out. I called this conference to tell you to shut up. No more interviews with government men. No more freelancing activities. This is bar-the-door time because the wraps must be put on."

"That's all right," Hurwitz says, reverting to type, feeling a white cloud of pallor engulf him. "I won't make any trouble at all."

"I wanted to advise you that there are very large stakes here and that certain risks may not be taken. If the federals come in again you are to refer them to me. You are to make no comment. And if necessary we'll retire you to get you out of the picture."

"All I wanted was a job," Hurwitz says. "A sense of efficiency, a kind of connection. Nothing more than that. I did not bargain for this."

"That's how it all begins," Marvin Martin says with enormous understanding. "First it's a job and then it's something else. I'd like to get you on as a participant. We could discuss this some more. Of course employees are not allowed and you're really not very interesting to me, Hurwitz. That's the trouble. No one interests me very much any more. Except Monaghan. Monaghan has promise. You stay out of this, Hurwitz. You get in between me and circumstance and things will be very unpleasant."

"All right. All right."

"There is nothing more here. Do you have anything to say?"

"I did not bargain for any of this. I have a master's degree. I wrote a thesis. I was on the way to a doctor of philosophy. Now Hurwitz feels that he bears no relation to what he was."

"That is an old problem of Americans. Stop referring to yourself in the third person. That's disassociation reaction."

"Hurwitz is tired," Hurwitz says and moves to the door. "He always did the best that he could. He did what he was expected to do. Now he is very tired."

"Perhaps something can be arranged."

"Everything," Hurwitz says, "has been arranged. There are no freelancers any more." He bows his head. He turns. He leaves the room and presence of Marvin Martin, saying no more. Behind him, airlessly, the door closes. In the reception room the secretary is looking with vast attention toward some of the twitches and gestures which Hurwitz makes on his exit but he pays her no mind. The secretary is an abstraction. The offices are an abstraction. Hurwitz is an abstraction. Only Marvin Martin is not; sunken in his corporeality he stays behind, sheltered by his desk, performing unspeakable acts with pencil and paper. Hurwitz thinks he can see him now, see the light of reason glowing in the Marvin Martin eyes as he sets pencil to paper, paper to desk, begins the Ultimate Memo in triplicate. The memo will filter through, processes will be continued, conclusions will be made. Hurwitz, alien to these surfaces as he would be to the moon, strides through airlocks and paneling, controlled environments and compression lockers, feeling the bulky weight of his guilt like a suit upon his back, the guilt funneling into his alien lungs the pure, thin taint of corruption, his private atmosphere, which will sustain him only a few hours longer in the terrain he cannot meet.

XXXI

Once Hurwitz had a wife and this wife said to him, "Don't touch me, don't you touch me now, get away from me. This will be the ruination of you, can't you understand what's happened? I can't take it any more; you don't even see what he is," and Hurwitz, not yet then divorced, had leaned over his wife in the sanctity of her bedroom and said, "See what? There's nothing to see. Can't you see my side of it; I'm fed up, I can't stand it any more, there's nothing to be done. It's just too large, too futile, you'll never change it, now I only want to get a piece of it myself so that I can be comfortable and save the private parts; isn't what we can build together important? doesn't that matter?" and she said, "The only private parts of yourself are what you want to put into me" and "There is nothing to build together if you can do this kind of thing to me," and Hurwitz said, "Do it to *you*? What about *me*? Do you think I like this? Do you think I don't realize that this is a compromise but there is work to be done and there's something going on in here; maybe it is possible to change the consciousness of Americans in this way, if you can show them what they are, if you can force them into an understanding of what they have become," and she said, "Don't you touch me, you son of a bitch, I can't stand you to touch me, just get away from me," and he said, "What the hell was I supposed to do, get a doctorate in sociology and spend the rest of my life working out a miserable living writing papers which no one will read and teaching people what they cannot understand," and she said, "It was what you wanted to do," and he said, "It wasn't what I wanted to do, not any more; I don't believe a word of it, there is no such thing as sociology, it's just a bunch of failed men talking jargon and using society as a projection of what went wrong in them inside," and she said, "I don't believe that, I don't believe you mean it," and Hurwitz said, "I do, I really do," and sought to mount his wife, his genitals inflated to enormous size by the passion of the argument or maybe it is only recrimination that Hurwitz retrospectively regards, "I believe every word of it and I'm glad I went to work at *Revelations* because now at last we will get into the matter of truth," and pounded himself into her massively, without flourishes, all purpose and direction to Hurwitz's functioning in those days and instead of fighting him she collapsed, let her body go slack, confronted him with flesh so mindless and empty that he could work himself upon it in suspension forever and entice no response, no response at all; this attitude of his wife's drove Hurwitz quite mad (in a certain way he has never gotten sane since) and he tried harder and harder to wring from her at least a cry but there was no cry, no sound from her, only a glance as level and empty as death and to his disgrace he came, feeble sputters and streams into her, unable to withdraw, helplessly pinned within his orgasm which he had to finish, chained within an orgasm which caused him to descend further and further (he is still falling) and when he removed himself he looked past her eyes and saw the wall and the wall was a screen and on the screen Marvin Martin was saying *it's time that we found out something about ourselves* and Hurwitz waited for the Revelation to come but then Marvin Martin laughed and laughed, his face changed to chalk in the wall and he pointed a finger, finger and face dissolving as Marvin Martin said, *and the beginning, Hurwitz, is with you* and Hurwitz poised himself forward, waiting at last for the knowledge to come, waiting for the words that would show Hurwitz to Hurwitz, confrontation forever (he is still listening; he is still waiting) and the image crumbled and turned to glass on the wall and drained away, Hurwitz drained away too and collapsed across his wife and there for all he knows, he lays still, locked in that posture, all of this that has happened since a dream (surely it must be a dream), a projection from the wrenching orgasm during which he saw a vision of Marvin Martin and thought that through Martin he would touch the sense of everything.

"I can't really take this," his wife said. "I'm going to have to leave you. It's been building for a long time but this is the final straw; I just don't see how we can make it together any more. I feel like a whore." She wiped his come from her cunt and went to the bathroom and when she came out she was in suit with baggage, waiting for the taxi to come which it did although Hurwitz is perhaps compressing events a little bit in what passes these days for his mind and most of this took considerably longer to happen.

XXXII

Dear Mr. Hurwitz:

I got the good news today that I had been accepted as a participant on the program *Revelations* and even in the excitement and happiness of the moment I did not want to forget to sit down to write you who are all but responsible for this a brief letter of thanks. It was very kind of you to listen when no one else would and now that I will have a chance finally to tell my whole story to the world so that they will understand what has been done to me you can be sure that you will not be forgotten and that I will mention you as well as the man most responsible for my salvation.

It is a great thing to know that at last you will have a chance to explain yourself so that people can see what you (I mean to say *I*) have been through over these past years (I am not confusing *you* with *me* and want to assure you that I understand and forever our personalities are inextricably different) and can make up their own minds. Deep in the television studios when the first landing on the moon was presented before an invited audience of high government officials and selected astronauts, we were talking about exactly things like this. "What would they say?" I remember one of my fellows asking, "what would John Q. say if he knew that all of this was a hoax and that we weren't near the moon but doing the whole thing in a studio as merely a means of taking attention away from the war and the failure of the government to help people understand their lives? Would they get mad? I bet that they would be merely disappointed that it had been taken away from them." I replied to him that it was not our responsibility to tell the public what was really going on since we were a select audience and employees of the agency and this astronaut (who has long since severed all connections with sanity and whose identity I therefore would not in fairness divulge) but that if we did I did not think that it would make any difference at all inasmuch as the public was getting exactly what it wanted and this astronaut, as I started to say, having somewhat lost the trend of my thoughts, and this astronaut said, "Well, I know what you mean but they ought to be told anyway if you have any faith left in old John Q.," and then we became very silent and quiet to watch as the simulated moon landing was conducted, all of it done so carefully and up to such high production standards that you could almost believe that you were on the moon if you know what I mean rather than in a basement in the testing grounds two hundred feet below the surface watching all of this going on. As we sat there we astronauts compared notes and tried to understand the technique of it very well because we would, some of us anyway, be the next people in the future to participate in this and it was important to see how it worked. The politicians watched it closely too but for different reasons. "We must do something about this," the astronaut next to me said, the one I have already mentioned, "we cannot let people live their lives in eternal ignorance, in a condition of being eternally lied to; there has got to be some coming-to-terms, the truth is the only thing that we've got after all. After all," this astronaut said, "if this goes on people won't be able to distinguish soon between their lives and their lies and then where will they be?" "Who gives a shit," someone else said and "cut it out; you're making waves," someone pointed out, and this astronaut (who was of course myself, haven't you figured that out by now? what a clever ploy that was) said no more but riveted his full attention on the events going on before him like events happening deep in the barrel of a microscope; inconsequential creatures performing imponderable acts and there was no more of that, no more that time although the astronaut kept on thinking and finally reached a point where the thought broke free.

Well, I seem to be wandering; that isn't exactly what I meant to do, of course, I wanted to stick right to the point and make this a simple thank-you note for having enough faith in me to grant me this opportunity but as seems to be more and more the case these days I relatively lost track of the point and kept on going to the right and left, to the side of it, compounding simple gratitude with irrelevant memory. I am very grateful to you for having the chance at last to square people away, so to speak, on what is going on. The fact that all of this is in the past and no one of my acquaintance seems to care about the agency any more is not the point because they will be *made* to care just as I was by subsequent events. I have gathered from certain sources which I cannot disclose that like me you had a wife and now are estranged from her. Don't worry about it, Mr. Hurwitz! Marriage is only a compound for guilt, this is something which I have come to understand. Without guilt there could be no marriages; without marriages there could be no guilt. Otherwise everything is fine and at the television studio, a quarter of a million miles out or what have you, I am at last pledged to give the reasons. With everlasting gratitude . . .

XXXIII

There are other applicants. A *castrati* in Detroit who was a circus juggler and a member of its freak show before settling down to being a physical education instructor is willing to explain how his lifestyle has been totally unaffected by his condition. A member of the Kansas state assembly has been tried for and acquitted of the murder of his second wife and wants to tell the whole story for the first time. A prostitute in Newtown, once a ballet teacher in a small midwestern community, knows exactly what drives customers to prostitutes and is willing to explore this. Three deformed brothers on salvage in New York City have a peculiar subterranean relationship which can be extracted for a price. A woman claiming to be a cousin of Marvin Martin says that she has interesting details on his background which *Revelations* might find exciting. (This one repels me totally and I set flame to it.) A retired brigadier general, who now receives messages from the National Security Alliance broadcast through his teeth, knows exactly why the recent war effort failed so totally and is willing to bring shocking facts to light for the first time. A prominent actress admits to being an out-of-wedlock child and in view of the renewed public interest in bastards is anxious to tell her warm, human story. A college social group in Canandaigua, New York, would like to appear *en masse* to discuss the latest sexual fads and follies in the colleges. A professional linebacker in the United Football Leagues maintains that a surprisingly large proportion of professional players have been rendered sterile or impotent by indiscriminate steroid dosage and although fans would be shocked to hear this he must reveal that the national sport is being played by people, a large proportion of which are in all but the medical sense of the term, *castrati*.

This seems to bring me full circle. Hurwitz passes on the juggler, denies the ballet teacher, has the brigadier written for a photograph, forwards the names of the three deformed brothers to the New York salvage agency for disciplinary action since they are seeking undeclared income while being public charges. Hurwitz processes, considers, certifies, denies, performing all of these actions with godlike ease, swooning facility, pallid nervous mannerisms which would indicate that externally at least nothing at all has changed. He is still the same. Hurwitz is always the same. Thus it would take the elf inside, the screaming, chanting, mad and melodramatic elf who runs free in the corridors to know the truth, the simple bare truth that not even *Revelations* could find: Hurwitz does not care any more. None of it matters to him. Hurwitz, A Man With A Passion, thinks only of Monaghan, thinks Monaghan all day, counts the weeks down to the segment when Monaghan will be taped. He does not know exactly why he is doing this. Perhaps he is thinking of something else. Perhaps he is imagining Hurwitz up there, deep in the machinery, cold as glass, translucent as diamonds, telling it all to Marvin Martin before the humming equipment while outside millions at last attend to this true and unique Hurwitz who at last will tell the Real Story.

XXXIV

"You're not involved with me at all," Doris Jensen says to me. "You're involved with some image of yourself you've projected on me. Hurwitz the Man Who Lives Dangerously, that's what I think it is. You're making love to yourself through the mirror that is me, that's all."

"You sound like my wife," I say. "You sound exactly like my wife," Hurwitz says and presses himself once again to Doris Jensen, feels her rise and fall against him, now spent with love juices but still active in reflex. Ah, Doris Jensen! "That was how she always sounded. Everything had to be analyzed."

"It's the truth."

"Enough introspection, analysis, idiosyncrasy! Simple acts for a simple man," Hurwitz says and seeks to bear her

89

down on the bed again, misses his aim, rolls off her rather clumsily and finds himself staring ceilingward, a cigarette suddenly poised in his hand which Doris Jensen lights with vast consideration. Thoughts of sex vanish from him, his prick sags, he blows rings of smoke. "I can't get over how it's going along," he says, his mind now on professional matters. "I never would have figured that it would have gone along this way."

"Who?"

"Monaghan."

"I don't want to hear about Monaghan any more. All I hear is discussions of Monaghan. If that's all that's on your mind I think you should get out."

"I can't," Hurwitz says. "It's too marvelous. You're too corrupt. You're what I've been waiting for all my life. Your thighs alone, your thighs, drive me to insanity." He presses the round, sagging flesh of the Jensen thigh, seeing it turn faintly bluish under the pressure, the rubric of veins winking at him through the impenetrable flesh and then moves his hand up to touch the Jensen cunt, feeling his come dribbling like insects through his fingers and onto the sheets. "Marvelous," he says, "to find this. It would be impossible for me to leave you, don't even think of it. Even though I know you're a spy for the competition and you're turning in everything I say to them. But I don't care. It's worth it. Everything's worth it." A vague quizzicality hits him, a feeling of unease. "Except Monaghan," he says. "I don't understand that."

"Don't mention him any more."

"That Marvin Martin would take him under his wing like that. It's uncanny. Usually he has nothing to do with participants until he gets them on tape, smack across the table. He calls them meat."

"Monaghan is a ridiculous little man and you want to emulate him."

"Marvin Martin is totally detached. Yet in Monaghan he takes a close interest, he even defends him against government intervention. This is inexplicable."

"I know you don't feel for me," she says, running her fingers over his stomach. "Ah," she says, letting the hand poise there, "ah God, I can feel all your thoughts running around inside there like little animals. Unbearable," she says and presses her lips to my stomach, "ah, it's unbearable, I can't stand it," and her breasts ring me, brushing across the stomach, moving down toward the groin, upward toward the face in a simultaneous swoop, incredible feat of contortion for Doris Jensen as with the same movement she manages to perform an unspeakable act upon those genitals which are now poised for entrance or destruction. She does what is necessary while Hurwitz lies back, makes the requisite pictures behind his closed eyes until a culmination, no matter how peripheral, has been reached. "If only you cared for me," she says, running her hands over the back of his neck, "how strange that would be."

"I do care for you. The monumental corruption of you. I am enticed, bewildered."

"I don't understand you."

"I don't understand you either," I say. "I don't understand any of it. I felt that I knew Marvin Martin. I felt that I understood how he works, how he feels; I felt often that I was inside him, could apprehend the mystery. But this is totally at variance. This is inexplicable."

"You sound unhappy."

"Unhappiness has nothing to do with it. Emotions are abstractions. Hurwitz is confused. He feels that somehow he is out of control."

"Why must you think about this?" she says, leaning across him, taking a cigarette. All pauses, all lapses in connection are sealed by cigarettes; this is an indication of the bad novel which Hurwitz's life has become. "Why can't you just be of the moment? Why is this on your mind?"

"Restlessness," Hurwitz says, "fundamental restlessness." He rolls over, faces Doris Jensen, her dangerously smoking cigarette inches from his cheeks. He and Doris Jensen have been lying in bed, inexhaustibly fucking, inexhaustibly tired, for several hours; still he cannot penetrate the mask of her flesh. This more than anything else is what he finds exciting. "I have a feeling," he says. "Just an apprehension."

"I don't want to hear about it."

"No, I don't care. Even if you are a spy and carrying back messages, Hurwitz does not care. He has now a rare, springing sense of disconnection from the consequences of his acts; nothing truly matters to him. Causation is vanquished."

"Talk English."

"You understand. You understand everything. I have an apprehension that matters are winding to a conclusion. They will not be the same again, they will forever be changed. The key is Monaghan."

"That little man? He does not matter."

"That's right, that's the point, that's exactly what I'm trying to say, he does not matter. He makes a virtue of inconsequentiality of irrelevance. Nevertheless he is there. He is merely a *ficelle*, as the good Henry James would say, but oh, what a *ficelle*! What a construction. I was slightly impotent before we met but since then everything's been fine."

"I'm glad."

"I'm glad too." Hurwitz takes the cigarette from her hand, wincing against the fumes, places it in an ashtray near the bed, still unextinguished (perhaps unextinguishable) and seeks to immerse himself in her once again, feeling the dark odors rising, the full thighs setting, the sagging breasts trembling; he buries himself in Doris Jensen seeking to yank out from himself yet one more response and finds himself saying, "Why don't we get married? We go so well together, it would be so right, so fitting, why don't we just go somewhere and get a certificate like anyone else?" and Doris Jensen laughs, she laughs and laughs, the cries coming from her like the sound of come and Hurwitz dives deeper, ever deeper, moving to the rotten core of her, the image of Monaghan remaining however cool and quiet in his mind during all of this; from that circle of stillness the cries come and he cannot stop them.

XXXV

SAUNDERS: I didn't run for President. My *brother* did.

MARTIN: You identified so strongly with your brother that you were actually participating in the campaign yourself. Here is an excerpt from your book, *My Brother and Me*, page 171: "As I grew older, I felt more and more that Harry and I were not two disparate people, two separate personalities, but were instead two sides of the same coin. He was the heads side, I the tails and time and again it was bottoms-down but I never doubted for a minute that basically we were the same and underneath it all I think that he felt that way too."

SAUNDERS: That was all ghost-written stuff. I didn't have much to do with it.

MARTIN: What if your brother had actually become President? Would you have been President as well in your own mind?

SAUNDERS: He didn't have much of a chance that year. Everyone knew that.

MARTIN: I have certain documents before me indicating that you applied for membership in the new-Nazi league. In a questionnaire submitted to that now-defunct organization you stated that your brother was a well-known politician and that you had complete control over him, would be able to use his influence to further the purposes of the league.

SAUNDERS: Where did you get those?

MARTIN: We get everything. Every goddamned thing. We have sources everywhere.

SAUNDERS: The hell with that.

MARTIN: You didn't really think that your record could be concealed, did you?

SAUNDERS: That was a long time ago. A very long time ago. Besides, no one really believed in the league. It was just something that the boys were getting into that summer.

MARTIN: What else were you getting into that summer, Saunders?

SAUNDERS: Huh?

MARTIN: Isn't it a fact that when your brother was in the statehouse you were using one of its back bedrooms as a rendezvous point for your shabby little affair . . . with his full knowledge and cooperation?

SAUNDERS: That's a dirty lie.

MARTIN: Oh God, this is so laborious. Laborious! Give me patience. Let's try to put it all together now, Saunders. Our time is running short.

SAUNDERS: Maybe your time is running short. I got a long way to go.

MARTIN: Watch your disgusting mouth before I lose my patience with you. We have, first, the identification with the brother, the Gordian knot of sibling attraction which can be traced back years, virtually from the birth of your younger brother three years behind you. We have this merging of psyches, this sense of over-dependency transferred from older to the favored younger in which the brother became the main element of your fantasy-life, an all-powerful figure who could act out your own avenging fantasies which dreams, oddly enough, originated from his very presence. From your hatred of him. We have that, firstly. Then, we have the indiscriminate sexuality, the coupling, the vagrant affairs, the loose and transitory marriages, the shoddy bouts with alcoholism, the simultaneous need of and tormenting assaults upon women which would sometimes be fused together in a transcendent sadism. We have the power-fantasies all tied up with the repressed homosexuality and hatred—

SAUNDERS: The what?

MARTIN: Let me finish! The power fantasies which were manifested by your membership in such organizations as the new-Nazi league, the love of hunting, fascination with guns, identification with figures of punishment evincing itself in your love of cowboy costumes, of wearing masks; we have all of these bound together, then, the hatred of the brother, the repressed homosexuality which came out of your very terrible need, doubtless for him, the dreadful need to resolve the conflict through murder and sadism and when we take these and fuse them together toward a final understanding of you, Saunders, do you know what we've got? Do you? Do you see what is going on?

SAUNDERS: No. No.

MARTIN: Do you see the total sum?

SAUNDERS: What is it?

MARTIN: The total sum is a lousy show! A stinker! An apostasy, a parody of what I one day dreamed! What has happened to all the participants, what has happened to the energy, the focus? Don't you sons of bitches care any more? I'm sinking! I'm a man sinking into his own waste and misappropriation! My vision, my talent, my courage, my intimation and look what you're turning it into! Whores, dilettantes, whiskey-assassins from the southwest! Get this man out of my sight! Run an old tape! Scrub the show, go back to the year one, what do I care? This is the last time, goddamn it, that I'll put up with anything like this and if this astronaut blows up on me next week I'll finish all of you. You'll never work another day in your lives, in or out of this industry if you do this to me. I've taken just about all that I'm ever going to take and now I'm drawing the line. You thought that I'd go on forever, didn't you, just moving along from week to week, never understanding, never caring, never coming to grips: you thought that I was so far out of the picture that you hacks and flacks and stewbums could get away with everything but you were wrong! This is my show, I created it! I seized it in the night, I shaped it like a jewel and I won't surrender it cheap. I am taking over! This is my show! Cut the tape.

SAUNDERS: What you were saying about me was very interesting. I never looked at things that way before. How'd you learn to think like that?

XXXVI

At the time of the first moon landing (was there a first moon landing?) Hurwitz was a multi-media executive. Far behind him were his academic days, somewhat ahead of him was *Revelations* and the time of dispute with his dear wife who still then considered him a man of large capacity, poised on the edge of worthwhile things. Hurwitz watched the moon landing in his bedroom at some horrendous hour of the morning, two hours later had to put together the small pieces of his psyche and venture into what was then Manhattan for an inevitable and not-to-be-cancelled conference. "Cataclysmic events come and go but life goes on," Hurwitz murmured to his dear wife and his d.w., head under the pillow, murmured that she understood this very well. "Have a good life," his d.w. said, which was their standard parting comment on mornings when something particularly portentous seemed to be in the offing, "and don't forget to clock in and out," and Hurwitz went on his way to the offices; three hours later he was embroiled in an argument over the best way to reach a large subculture of adolescents in Toledo, Ohio, who were considered to be more or less typical of the larger subculture of American adolescents everywhere. Certain elements felt that it was necessary to map out a campaign which would enable the adolescents to define themselves as miniaturizations of their parents, their needs being catered to in terms of their parent's obsessions, but a minority, of which Hurwitz was a leading member, felt that the dislocation and alienation of almost all aspects of youth was complete and the most intelligent campaign would be one to admit to the potential buyers that they were an entirely different class altogether and work on the basis of their independence. The argument became progressively vicious—the product at issue was a soap which would cause large facial pores to contract or at least to appear minimized—and at one point Hurwitz found himself rising to his feet, roaring to his full height (he was then a thin and graceful one hundred and seventy pounds, being held in place by necessity and tension) and saying, "What the hell does it matter any more? Must we eternally trivialize everything? Men have landed upon the moon this morning, the moon being the only piece of holy ground that Americans can understand and yet in the face of this, in the face of the largest act we have known in our lifetimes we continue to hash over this nonsense as if nothing had changed. Stop it! Stop it!" this younger, minimized Hurwitz shouted and there was something of a silence; after a few moments consoling hands were placed around his waist and neck and he was led from the room by experienced voices who told him that he had come up with something, he had really come up with something there but he was, perhaps, a bit over-wrought and could do with something of a break. Hurwitz had a break, he had a long break in the men's room and subsequently in a delightful bar tucked into a corner of the lobby; it occurred to him not for the first time that he could quit his job but purpose seemed to fold into him as he sat over the martinis: thinking of the brave, arching backs of the astronauts as they had clambered liked animals over the surfaces of the moon, he guessed that he was as capable of taking risks in the face of such courage as anyone and besides he had certain coverages through the pension plan; the refund on his paid-in benefits alone could carry him for several months and then too his wife was employed as a statistical researcher. "I'll do it, I'll really do it; I could do no less on Moon Day," the slightly drunken Hurwitz muttered to himself and ascended with one of the martini glasses all the way to the thirtieth floor, walked past the receptionist, past batteries of bookkeepers and into the conference room where the meeting was still ongoing and where it turned out that in Hurwitz's absence a campaign had been worked out to incorporate the moon landing into the policies of the campaign at issue. The campaign at issue had been a contract with the Pentagon to induce teenagers to volunteer for the armed services, and the moon landing, being both inspirational and highly military, seemed to lend itself well to posters and action-blowups. "That's the key," Hurwitz was told by some of his associates, superiors and co-workers, "I think that you've given us the twist to the whole campaign," and Hurwitz allowed himself the luxury of leaving the room and being very sick down the hall but there was an overlay of melodrama to his vomiting and all through regurgitation Hurwitz could not stop thinking that he was acting like certain admirable characters in novels which he had once read. (This is no longer his problem; not for many years now has Hurwitz thought of himself as a character in a novel, even a bad one.) He knew even then that he would not quit, that the act of vomiting itself was as far as he needed to go with gestures of renunciation.

On the train home, in the club car, Hurwitz thought of the events of the day, thought of the moon: there were the men bouncing on those awful surfaces, the long-range cameras imparting a dreadful portentousness to their simple acts through slow motion, all of these hops and manipulations seeming to take place through layers of water, and wondered if his life had been irrevocably changed because men had landed on the moon. He did not think that it had been; the fact that he was living at a time when the landing was made seemed purely coincidental like certain Roman peasantry during the time of Jesus who were aware of vague stirrings in the marketplace. What Hurwitz was doing he could have done at any time or place; there was no question of being ennobled by events captured in the public sphere. He found himself deep in conversation in the club car eventually with a thin, intense man who said that the landing was the perfect circular key to the decade; the assassinations and the landing that was, they were the same thing, acting in consort together toward a perfect vision of what had happened to the country what with murder becoming merely a routine public event and the landing, symbolically, becoming murder; the thin intense man said that he was stalking a theory which was not quite ready for articulation yet but had something to do with the fact that public events had only one function and that function was the commentary they caused; the more inventive journalism or advertising they could evoke, the more significant they were; actually all events existed in a void where they were equally insignificant with everything coming after the fact through commentary but of course this theory was a little bit rough yet and he didn't want to push it as hard as it might eventually be taken. The thin, intense man turned out to be Marvin Martin, then a local newscaster working under the name of Timothy Waite but no more need be said of that since it occurs out of its proper place and this earlier meeting with Marvin Martin/Timothy Waite has absolutely nothing to do with events as they progressed.

XXXVII

Hurwitz taking his ease in his apartment, Hurwitz lying around in robe and lounging equipment, puttering around the unfurnished rooms, drinking a little scotch on a free night, even turning from time to time to these very notes which have become a noxious, spilling agglomeration of paper over this desk. (I did not realize when I began this the depth of my obsession; how I would insist upon getting everything down, how no detail would evade my grasp, the urge for scholarship postponed fifteen years seems to be oozing out of every pore; now *everything* must be put down on paper. This was supposed to be a shy, impressionistic chronicle of My Life With Revelations, suitable for display at conventions or as an icebreaker at a party; how did I get in this deep? What do I have to prove? What precisely do I think I have in mind as I drive on, drive on through levels and levels of recollection, opinion, complaint? This is an old question; I do not deign to answer.) Hurwitz sealed off for once from this world if not the memory of it, listening to distant music upon his record player, watching the evening light come through his windows as he sits in the dark and plays with recollection. Memory assaults him, recollection, sentiment, yet the memory is, for once, without feeling; he is able to dispassionately examine his past, make certain calculations, come to certain viewpoints without ethos and this informs him with a vast sense of peace. Life, that lunatic game, no longer seems unbearable to Hurwitz as he takes his apartment ease; it does not seem strictly bearable either but somewhere between impossibility and adjustment Hurwitz thinks that he can mediate. His belly trembles, jowls tremble, eyes blink and water, fingers fly over the papers as he adds an occasional note; Hurwitz is as close to accommodation as he will ever come. Witness him. It will be for the last time.

One moment there is silence, music pouring from the speakers, the whisk of pencil over paper: the next there is a dismal rattle at the door, tentative knocks, the sound of heavy breathing. Hurwitz's first thought is of prowlers: prowlers come often to his apartment building in the west eighties, seeking precious objects from the tenants of this building, not understanding that whatever is truly precious to them was sacrificed decades ago, can no longer be found in these reconstructed apartments. Nevertheless there is a dim history frantically concealed by the building management: raids, assaults, a bloody battle on the stairwell, an old lady found too peaceful in her bed by disinterested chambermaids days later. These apprehensions inform Hurwitz with powerful fears; archetypes spring from the husk of the night and assault him with nibbling little teeth. "Who's there?" Hurwitz says. There is snaffling in the hallway, thumping, a discouraged bounce or two and Hurwitz, summing the remnants of his courage (when he is killed, he wishes to confront the assassin face to face, this is why he admires Marvin Martin) wobbles to the door, removes the chain, tears open the door and confronts the hallway. "All right," he says into the darkness, inhaling what he thinks may well be his last foul breath of air, "all right, what do you want? Who is it?"

His eyes blink in the darkness, focus, readjust (Hurwitz, it must be confessed, has had more than a few drinks; this may explain his rather melodramatic cast) and a figure appears before him. The figure shakes itself into view-range, looks at Hurwitz, looks past him, looks into the apartment. "Oh God," the figure says, "may I come in?" It is Walter Monaghan.

"What are you doing here?" Hurwitz says. His contact with Monaghan has been minimal since the interview; there has been a little correspondence here, a refused phone call there but nothing to explain this visit in the guise of an assassin. "What do you want?"

"Talk," Monaghan says. "I want to talk. I've come here to talk. Won't you please let me in?" The question is unnecessary; Monaghan has already proceeded into the apartment. Hurwitz has a vivid fantasy, it reels itself out before him: Monaghan will turn in one motion, lunging, gigantified; he will fall upon Hurwitz like an archangel, he will rend Hurwitz from limb to limb, leaving only bleeding, guilt-stricken pieces around the apartment and when he is quite done with that (it will not be too difficult, Hurwitz is physically weak and is held together only by the most useless kind of wire) he will seize the Hurwitz possessions, the Hurwitz credentials and flee into the night, carrying with him forever the mortal remains of the tenant of the apartment. The apartment itself will be boarded up under the rent-control laws and eventually enshrined but this will all be too late to do Hurwitz any good. "Please," Hurwitz finds himself saying, reacting with profound woe to his speculations, his best audience always, "please don't," and turning to confront the assassin with what little dignity he has remaining finds Monaghan cuddled embryonically in a chair. The assassin has become a fetal object, shrunken upon himself; quite helpless he submits himself to Hurwitz's penetrating gaze which under these happy circumstances becomes quite awesome. "I just want to talk," Monaghan says. "You were the only person I could think of. I knew where you lived; I picked that up somewhere. They don't hardly let me go anywhere, they have me under wraps and I can barely make a move but tonight I decided I couldn't stand it any more; I just can't take it, I had to get out. You're the only person I can talk to, please let me talk. Just for a minute. Then I'll go; I promise that whatever happens I'll go but they just won't let me breathe any more."

"I don't think we have any business," Hurwitz says. "As far as I can see our involvement is finished."

"Don't I know that?" Monaghan says. "Don't you think I know everything. I know it isn't your fault, you did the right thing but what has happened—"

"What's happened?"

"Can I stay? Can I talk?"

"I don't know," Hurwitz says, moving to the door, closing the door, shutting off the music on the speakers which has moderated during Monaghan's entrance from a medley of show tunes to a rather dismal pastiche of Wagner's Greatest Hits. "I mean you're here, aren't you? But I don't see any point or purpose in this."

"Oh," Monaghan says, unresponsively, "oh, terrible things. You just couldn't imagine what terrible things are going on. They keep you in this room, this one room, you see, which is soundproofed and they bring you your meals and it's all supposed to be voluntary on your part because you're going to be a participant in the show and it's to your advantage that nothing happens to you in the very important week before the taping but there are voices, always there are voices coming through the loudspeakers which are part of the room and I think that they talk to you in your sleep and they say the most terrible things. Can I take off my coat? It's awfully warm in here; you must keep it at eighty degrees proper. It's just like the capsule used to get on the last day in; dense and odorous. Of course if you want me to—"

"No," Hurwitz says, leaning his back against the door, regarding Monaghan, "no, that's all right. You can take off your coat if you want to." From this distance he regards Monaghan rather carefully; Monaghan has certainly deteriorated in appearance or maybe it is only Hurwitz's vision of the world which is deteriorating (more and more to his disenchanted eyes the world seems to be the back edges of a used car lot); he is both smaller and more ponderous than as last recollected and is unshaven, three or four days worth of beard fighting for his complexion along with a series of uneven white patches which streak him along the nose and chin line. He has the aspect, Monaghan does, of an astronaut ready for retirement, of course he is considerably further along the line than that but the metaphor sticks, Hurwitz having never had personally much use for astronauts over and above any sense of professional involvement. It occurs to Hurwitz that this is the first time he has seen a *Revelations* participant between the time of initial interview and the appearance on the program; once or twice, it is true, he has seen some of the participants long after they have been on the air and a strangely reduced and shambling lot they are, but this is explicable, the Marvin Martin process being what it is. He had not been aware however that the deteriorative aspects began even before they had faced the cameras and an idea occurs to him: perhaps less credit should be given to the penetrating and deadly questions of Marvin Martin and more to the induction of certain powerful drugs into the bloodstream. It is certainly something to think about and Hurwitz resolves that he will bring his full attention to bear upon it, his best ideas having always occurred to him in brief, odd flashes, impacted and without prelude. He begins to wonder, in fact, if *Revelations* might indeed be somewhat manipulated, a possibility which has actually never occurred to him before. "Terrible things," Monaghan is saying meanwhile, now divested of his coat which collapses in a lump at his feet, wearing a streaked blue suit with certain medallions and ornaments which can only be the signatures of the agency, "oh, if I could only tell you what they did but you're part of the system too, I know that, I can't tell you a thing and besides you know already. Don't you, Hurwitz?"

"I don't understand," Hurwitz says. "I have no idea what you're talking about."

"Terrible," Monaghan says. "Oh God, should I open up and try to talk to you? On the one hand I desperately need to talk to someone. On the other hand, I'm sure that you're part of the cabal. I know it. Oh God, please, please, don't let them get me!" he shrieks and retracts into a pitiful huddle somewhere at Hurwitz's knees, Hurwitz thinks of paranoid schizophrenia and dissociative reactions but it only turns out to be a case of keener hearing because there are another series of shattering bumps at the door and then a man enters, wearing a long over-coat, his face tight and set underneath an expressionless hat. He looks vaguely familiar and Hurwitz perceives with a rush of memory that it is his old friend of two Fridays ago, ball-bearings. "All right," ball-bearings says, looking at Monaghan with a familiar and loving expression. "Come along."

"You see what I mean?" Monaghan says, huddling tighter into the Hurwitz couch-cushions. "Do you see what I mean? Do you?"

"There's no time for discussions," ball-bearings says. "You know perfectly well you shouldn't be running all over the city at this hour. It's time for bed."

"They don't let me sleep. I can't sleep. They come to me in the night and do things. Things with lights and noises."

"He's over-excited," ball-bearings says to Hurwitz with a wink. "They all get that way when they're going to be on television. Don't I remember you from somewhere? I think I seen you around."

"Please," Monaghan says, now curled up tightly, a man inside himself, holding a pillow, barricaded into a corner of the couch. "Don't let them get me. I can't take it any more. Someone has got to help. All right, I'll make a deal; help me and I'll tell you everything."

"I'm sure I seen you around," ball-bearings says with a shrug, moving to the couch and pulling Monaghan to his feet in a single, expert motion, causing Monaghan to gasp only slightly as some kind of pressure is applied. "Of course I could be wrong. I got a very bad memory for faces and besides that I got to concentrate on my work."

"Aren't you going to say anything?"

"Look," Hurwitz says, showing his palms, moving his palms outward and down, "it's not my affair. You understand that."

"You're going to let him just take me away without even listening?"

"I'm sorry," Hurwitz says. He knows that he is. "I'm not responsible. I just procure the talent, I have nothing to do with situations after that."

"Sure I remember you," ball-bearings says. "It all comes back to me now. The other day. Well, it doesn't matter; the important thing is to keep things on an even keel and get you home to bed." He gives Monaghan a tap which might be affectionate under the circumstances. "Some of them get difficult," he says to Hurwitz, as if he were walking Monaghan through a judging-ring. "Nervous about the whole thing and so on. You'd be amazed some of the things they go through. Of course he's no problem at all; he's taking things like a real pro. You're just a little nervous, aren't you, Walter?"

"I can't stand it any more," Monaghan says. "I can't stand it." He seems to revert to some more basic stage of existence, perhaps on an instinctual level bits and pieces of training come back to him; he crouches, allows his face to go blank with the aspect of a Man On A Training Mission, then attempts to slip ball-bearing's grasp and makes a small, potentially deadly maneuver with his left hand. Ball-bearings smiles, sighs, shrugs (in that suspended instant of time he is able to do all of this and more yet: ever more), looks sidewise at Hurwitz and then brings a hand down on Monaghan's neck, a small, absent chop which is more like a caress and Monaghan folds underneath him, would collapse if not held by the sudden support of another hand, hangs against ball-bearings for a long, dreaming instant and then subsides with a moan while Hurwitz, a physical coward, looks upon this scene; backs off a tread or two, examines Monaghan and says in the quietest of peeps, "was that strictly necessary?" stopping right then and there as Monaghan, locked deep into some distant connection, begins to moan about lights and lockers and probes and drugs, his voice alternately booming and quiet, coming in slow waves as if heard in the last instants before sleeps and ball-bearings says with a wink, "I'll take him off the premises now."

"No," Hurwitz says, "you don't understand." Ball-bearings says, "I understand perfectly, I understand everything perfectly; we're friends, right? I can count on it," and extends a hand, stands there in the light, Monaghan poised against him like a child and Hurwitz seizes the hand or is he merely dreaming this last part, extends a hand and they touch in a springing clasp, the flesh of ball-bearings cold and hard but with faint pinpoints of warmth buried within and then the two of them leave, ball-bearings and Monaghan that is to say, leaving Hurwitz quite alone in his unfurnished three and a half, the needle of the stereo set still scratching dumbly through the unamplified grooves, Hurwitz sighs, goes to the set, turns it off completely, the room now resonant with silence and remembers Monaghan's last words to him as he had half-staggered, half rode from the room, "this has got to stop," Monaghan had said with a horrid confidentiality, just mouthing the words, Hurwitz picking it up as if from the walls, "this can't go on any more, there has to be an end to it, make an end to it, Hurwitz, make an end to it," or was Hurwitz merely dreaming all of this too, dreaming this and ball-bearing's handshake, the clasp, the gasp, the admission, the pact, all sealed in his dreams and the only events in the room simple barbarism and abduction? Hurwitz does not know; a long time ago he abducted himself for a hillside where he could perch without the need for judgments of any sort. He has sat on that hillside for a long, long time now, has Hurwitz and he has never, even at this moment, been impelled to question his choice. It is just the way things are; it is the way things have worked out. Hurwitz never did less than the necessary. He never did any more either.

Nevertheless, even though it is strictly not necessary he locks his door, double-bolts his door, leaves a message with his answering service that if he is not heard from by dawn they are to call the police (this is a celebrity service; nothing whatsoever disturbs them) and with the lights on lies on his bed for a while trying to make some sense of the events of the evening. Sense will not come; neither will sleep, and right up to almost the present moment Hurwitz lies on his bed, Hurwitz is lying on his bed, Hurwitz is moving around slowly on his bed, his gestures like a man trapped underwater or an infant swimming slowly in that first of all places, flexing his limbs against the unspeakable time to come.

XXXVIII

"Yes," Hurwitz says, now soothed, his head lying on Doris Jensen's breast, "yes, let's get married. Let's get married today. Why not? We're both unencumbered."

"I'm afraid you don't understand," she says. "We can't get married. Not ever. It would be a relationship of corruption, one bringing out the unhealthiest parts of ourselves."

"Why do women always talk like that?"

"It has nothing to do with sex. It's true. Besides, we can't possibly get married because I don't want to see the likes of you any more."

"What's that?" Hurwitz says, disengaging himself, moving to leave a small abscess between them on the bed, then returning with a cigarette and a new sense of purpose. "I don't understand what you're saying."

"I said I won't be seeing you any more. There's no point to it. It's gone as far as it can go and now I want to look for something else."

"That's a terrible thing to say."

"Call me fickle. I've never been able to have a stable relationship. I go along for a while and then I look for someone or something else. I'm always seeking. A doctor I used to talk to a long time ago said that it was a kind of self-hatred and I was constantly changing objects because I could not bear myself."

"Don't give me that nonsense," Hurwitz says, touching a flabby upper arm, feeling the flesh curl familiarly into his fingers, wandering his fingers down to an open hand which he brings across to caress his genitals. "That psychological stuff. I don't believe a word of it any more. You're saying this because you just want to bring things to an end and you're interpolating all this business."

"If you say so."

"I won't have it. If you want to break something off you do it honestly and on its own terms. You don't quote absent sources, dead platitudes."

"If that's the way you want it. I mean it though. I really do. The whole thing is too sick. I can't stand it any more."

"I don't believe you," Hurwitz says. He tries to light the cigarette, finds the matches dead, puts all of this beside him on the nighttable, meanwhile midnight streaks of sirens and panic work their way in through the windows. There seems to be the sound of a sudden beating outside, cries, flight in the night, random curses hurled from windows, all part of the west nineties secret. "I don't think that that's the reason at all and I think that you're holding back on me."

"If you say so."

"Orders from above?"

"Whatever you say."

"I can't stand this goddamned inference business!" Hurwitz says loudly. "Everything is misdirection, incomplete, stultified, cut off. No one in any branch of the business seems to come out and say what he means! I'm sick of the whole thing, I tell you that. Can't we talk some sense here?"

"If you please. I'd rather not talk sense. I'm tired and it's time for you to leave. Remember, we agreed that you would never stay all night."

"I want to finish this," I say with monomaniacal eagerness, "just once I want to see this through. I want things to be said, to be out in the open. Can't you understand that?"

"I didn't want you to get involved. You knew how it was from the first; what it was going to be. You did it to yourself but you can't say that I didn't play fair with you."

"You hooked me in," I say. "You and Monaghan, you both came along at the same time, the two of you. Your job was to keep me quiet and peaceable when Monaghan came onto the scene and above all to keep me talking. You were relaying information; everything that I said was getting back to someone else. But now that Monaghan is scheduled and things are being wound up, it's time to cut me off."

"That's a very paranoid series of assumptions. I'm not sure that I want to discuss any of that right now."

"It's out in the open. Isn't it time that things got right into the open? I tell you, I don't understand the language any more! I can barely speak it. I have no tolerance for this!"

"I'm sorry, Hurwitz, I think that you should go now." She has never called me by my first name, it has always been

Hurwitz, the business relationship permeating through to the last sighs of orgasm when she has muttered, *oh Hurwitz, you can do it*. "We can talk it over some other time."

"Bitch," I say, rearing up in the bed. "Bitch, take off the mask. I've never seen you, not for a moment. Take it off; let me confront you." I reach toward her; whether assault or connection is on my mind I do not know but something happens to her face, something hard and perilous and I back off from her, under the seizure of her eyes. Not since the first time am I ever able to make her break. "Get out," she says. "This is the finish. Get out now."

"I wanted to make you understand. I thought that if I could make one person understand it would be different. That was all. Monaghan meant nothing; I would have told you anything about him without being asked. You didn't have to do all the other stuff to hear me. I would have told you anyway."

"I don't want you to come back here," she says. "Take your things and leave. You are never going to come into this apartment again; I'll wait with knives if you do." She stands, moves to the window, wrapping various pieces of clothing like armor around her as she does so, moves slowly toward the window, turns then and looks at me. "You're too corrupt," she says. "You're too far gone. I can't handle you. It's just beyond me."

"I thought that about you."

"I don't want to hear what you have to say. Just leave. Leave before I do something terrible."

"Contrived," I say, standing as well and beginning to assemble my clothing from chairs, from tables, from the floor, "the whole thing is contrived. The rage doesn't work. You made it all up, didn't you?"

"Just get out of here."

"Your thighs, your cunt, your mouth, all of that was made up too. There was nothing in it at all. I thought that it was there; it was corrupt, it was narrow, it was painful but there was something. You have no idea how long Hurwitz has gone without feelings of any sort, feelings that is, that were anything other than fear. The butterfly on the pin. The frog on the electrodes. Stimulus-response, touch nerve and jump. There was something else here. I thought I saw it. I thought that I could; I did." I can sense tears in my voice. Tears in the voice of Hurwitz! "And there was nothing," I say. "Nothing at all. A continuing blankness."

"I'm very moved."

"It was manipulation, all the time: manipulation and inference. That's all."

"I won't have this any more," she says. "All my life I've been standing in small rooms, telling men that I won't have any more. Now I mean it. Stop torturing me. Stop torturing yourself. Get out of here."

"I wouldn't have anything to do with you," I say, "even if I were a man with options. I wouldn't touch you from a distance. I despise you. I renounce you."

"Renounce and get out for God's sake."

"I see that the knife-edge of your corruption turns both ways. There's nothing there. Nothing. Tell them all this. Tell them what I said to you."

"There is no them."

"Go on back to the top and say that you completed your mission with Hurwitz. That you've broken him."

"Oh, stop being so damned melodramatic," she says, turning and sitting on the bed in a languid posture, a certain ease now coming off her along with twinkles of light through the pain. "You're insanely paranoid and you don't even know how to plot. You're just a pitiful little man."

"Thank you," Hurwitz says. Hurwitz goes to the door, touches it with a painful and loving grasp. "I'll always remember that. That's the part of you I want to take with me forever. Show your breasts; angle just a bit more in profile and I'll see them forever."

"Go to hell," she says, "there's too much pain." Hurwitz leaves it at that, goes out the door, closes the door, terminates the relationship so to speak. Hurwitz has never had a graceful or easy hand at terminating relationships. Also (this is a secret confessed herein for the very first time, take note) most of his relationships have been ended for him, Hurwitz having been canceled out, so to speak, by women who have decided that they have moved past the point of possibility. It is conceivable that someday Hurwitz may actually initiate an action like this himself but if he does so it will be (alas!) for the very first time. Hurwitz will say no more.

Hurwitz will say no more about the Doris Jensen question. I have still not revealed her name. Now I never will. I will not mention her in these notes again after these sections. She will plummet out of my life like a meteorite, like an imploded spaceship. If I had the time I would go through these notes with a careless pencil, knocking out all reference to her, any indication that she ever existed. I do not have to dignify her; I could say all along that I had been fucking an abstraction, masturbating upon thin, thin air.

Only one last thought occurs to me before I refuse to dwell on her for all time: I always identified her somehow with the extrinsic, with menacing, threatening forces from outside, with the competition, so to speak, with the anti-*Revelations* crowd. What if, on the contrary, she had been employed by Marvin Martin (after the initial fiasco of her appearance because, at least, he felt that he could admire her) to keep tabs on *me*? I cannot put this beyond the man although I think that this would essentially have been cunning in a void, cunning without reference.

On the other hand, it might have suited Marvin Martin's purposes no less than anything else that he has ever done to me. (I have not begun to tell you and now do not have the space to tell you what he has done to me.)

I can see that I am becoming increasingly paranoid.

Hurwitz sees the world as a knife, descending dully upon a table top where he skitters, small helpless object, looking for protection in the eaves of a loaf of bread. It is too bad; Hurwitz in his youth did not believe that they were all out to get him, not until he would get them first. Chronology seems to reverse the balance.

I will try not to think any more of this. There is no point to it, no profit. Other things are on my mind. Things like Monaghan.

Only two days now before the taping. Why am I so conscious of this?

XXXIX

Dear Jennifer:

You may well be surprised to hear from me and in such a way after these many years but you have been on my mind recently and I thought, well no times like old times, and decided that I would write to your last known address and take my chances. I realize that you remarried some time ago (congratulations, I wish you much happiness) and went overseas but on the other hand the new private postal service is very prompt and efficient and maybe they will manage to find a forwarding address and get this in your hands. In any event, it is certainly time that we were in touch and I hope that you are the same and will perhaps keep me in mind.

Things are strange, Jennifer, you cannot understand how strange they have become. I am still working for *Revelations* as you threatened but think my tenure is coming to an end. I am trying to keep my thoughts and feelings in a simple one-line format and not to scatter them all over the paper but it is hard, hard; I have been keeping a journal recently which is not of the most organized kind and my thoughts and recollections seem to have spilled out onto the paper, so to speak, without a great deal of rhyme and reason and very much out of synchronization. This is a new way of thinking to me, as you are well aware, a man who always prided himself upon his neatness and sense of organization but I am not sure that it is deteriorative; life cannot easily be contained in schedules, chronology or timetables after all and there is an entirely different way of looking at the mystery as I have discovered. Maybe I should have been less organized years ago although this is a hell of a time to get into that question.

As I say, I am keeping this journal. In fact, I am keeping it at this very moment; I have not been doing anything much for the last couple of weeks other than working on this journal and participating (usually as a witness) in an amazing series of events in my private life: events which have to do with both the romantic and pragmatic sides of life but which are equally disastrous. At a certain point however I have heaved the journal away or at least have pushed it firmly to one side and have embarked instead upon this letter to you hoping that in so doing and so writing I will be able to make sense of these events which are largely so confusing. You were always very good for me in that way, Jennifer: you were a sensible person (until the last months when you became completely unreasonable but this is a friendly letter without any recriminations, as you will see) and helped me to feel that the world was ordered, kindly, and responsive; maybe through writing to you I will begin to feel that way again although I am not exactly sure of this and like so many others am merely stumbling around in the dark, trying to put the pieces together and wondering if my destiny is as uncertain as my origins.

There is an astronaut named Monaghan (remember the astronauts, Jennifer? It seems a long, long time ago but perhaps you will recall how we used to watch the early landings together, pausing in the midst of landscape for a bit of a fuck, blending exploration and scatology together in a wonderful midnight way which made us feel that we were part and parcel of the mission . . . of course astronautics has not been what it was for a long time now and I pity our younger people who did not, as we did, grow up as young adults with such a wonderful background) who appears to have been the twenty-ninth man on the moon. He is scheduled for participation in a *Revelations* format just two days hence (I have just checked my watch); I mean tomorrow. He is a strange man: tortured, demented, he claims that he is no longer affiliated with the agency because he was dismissed with prejudice and now that this has happened to him he wishes for the first time to sit down with Marvin Martin under lights and in the machines and tell America exactly what kind of agency has been hiding from them for all these years. This is not the important part, although I wish it were, and it has touched off a whole series of events and speculations both in and outside of Hurwitz which have placed me in very serious trouble and which I want to discuss with you. Now having said all of that I don't know if I have made it clear; I am trying to write this as levelly and simply as possible and with the exception of the one *Hurwitz* right above have not lapsed into the third person even once, a habit to which I am more and more prone these days as I sink deeper into dissociative reaction. (I know what dissociative reaction is, you see, Jennifer. I always knew far more than you gave me credit for knowing but we will not argue that now.)

Revelations has changed in the past few years; *Revelations* is not quite the program that I thought it was. In the first place it is clearer and clearer that Marvin Martin is not so much interested in his announced purposes of knowledge as he is in playing a very dangerous, destructive game with the participants and in the second place, as the initial novelty of the format has worn off, something has changed at the center of the program: it is nastier, harder-edged, possibly more dangerous, certainly more destructive and vicious. (Putting this down I have a feeling that I sound naive. Pardon that, I do not mean to sound naive: I merely wish to place some acts on the record. You are not a television person, Jennifer, you never were, and I want to fill you in as an outsider on what has been going on.) The purposes of the program seem less informational than barbaric; time and again Marvin Martin has used the format only to reduce participants (who are now occasionally called *contestants*; I think that this should give you an idea) to shattered masks who, shambling parodies of themselves, seem barely capable of human speech by the time that he is ready of them. I do not like what the format has become. You must believe that; I never thought that it would turn out this way and if I had seen it, I would not have stayed with it this long and until all my options are exhausted. You must believe this, Jennifer. I am not a cruel or sadistic person; I do not believe in the public humiliation of innocent people (even that corrupt garden-variety kind of innocent who appears on *Revelations*). Even if they are all recruited but eat agencies as I have come to believe, are put up to the matter by

cleverly concealed public-relations agents, they are still entitled to be treated with civility and respect. This is not the way
things should have ended. I believe this passionately.

(A thought occurs to me as I write this; perhaps, unknown
to me, all of the contestants are professional actors and are
merely performing roles with the eagerly collaborative
Martin. This is impossible; I cannot accept it. Even if so, the
pain is real and people are being taught all over the country that assault is equated with insight, fragmentation with
revelation. This is not the way that I would care to view the
human condition.)

There is an astronaut. His name is Monaghan. He claims
that the space agency has lied about all the moon expedi-
tions, no, that is not quite true; he tells a number of weird
and conflicting stories which do not seem to make any sense
when considered with any consistency: he says that all of
the moon flights were conducted in a television studio, he
says that several of the men on the flights went insane, he
said that the moon, when he landed upon it, was not made
of green cheese. Am I being coherent? He talks of lights and
probes and drugs in the night. He talks of being kept impris-
oned prior to his appearance. Two nights ago he came and
begged my assistance. I did nothing and he was taken away
from me.

I do not understand what is going on. Do you remember the summer we had in Berne, Jennifer? We were much
younger then and I was on an assistantship at the institute,
supposed to be studying the modal variations of behavior
among deviant groups in the inner cities in the first decade
of the century, but enough of that didactic nonsense; I would
be home from the library at ten in the morning and we
would sit overlooking the cliffs and drink wine; by noon we
were somewhat drunk and made love then on the balcony,

after that it was time for lunch and long discussions of what I would make of our lives (it was always what *I* would do; was this the problem, Jennifer?) and we would go bicycling or walking in all that greenery, all that damned greenery and space to the right and left of us, running down the slopes like animals and then back to the apartment and more sex, more love, perhaps a little wine, the slow dreamy coalescence we made upon those sheets set up barriers that I thought could hold against anything. Dinner. We would go to cafés and announce our plans to strangers who were drunker than us. Then we would come home. Perhaps there was more sex. Perhaps not. It is difficult to remember. Holding in the night I could see a vision; the vision was clearer than any I have had since and I had it all the time that summer: that I would come to a time of sanity and resting and the world would be locked out. Everything seemed possible that summer. The assistantship expired and our plans to stay there fell through and we came back, to the University of Iowa, I believe it was. Three years later I became a multimedia executive. It was not my fault. I would rather have been in Berne.

I do not understand any of the things that have happened to us. How did it wind up this way? More and more, I feel like a participant on *Revelations* myself; I start with a long, logical *precis*, a summary, really, of my condition; I am superbly balanced, totally logical, I only want a chance to explain, given that chance I can make a final order of my existence; I sit there calm, faintly pallid but otherwise possessed, reasonably explaining my life away and then the Questions begin; they are gentle at first, just probing at the layers, so to speak, asking for particulars of biography, to clear up inconsistencies of background; still superbly rational I answer those Questions, then the other Questions begin: my philosophy of life is inquired into, my point of view on existence, certain embarrassing personal details are hinted; soon the pallor has turned into a flush, the quiet and brilliantly controlled demeanor into a series of stammers and twitches, the Questions come thicker and faster and there I am still pinned on the chair, now I see lights, hear the whir of machines, become conscious of business in the background, shouts, movement, the bellows of technicians; still, I attempt to answer, one must be controlled, one must after all be reasonable, but the Questions pelt thicker and faster, now I am not sure of anything, slowly the senses begin to go, first that of touch fading into disconnection, then smell so that all my tortured nose gathers in is an impression of heat, then taste and sight are gone too and all that is left is hearing; hearing I will have forever and still the unanswerable Questions after all of this come: what are you doing, Hurwitz? what did you intend? do you really think that you can be spared responsibility for this? and so on and so forth and soon there is very little left of Hurwitz indeed: just a stuttering, quivering wreck moving on the vestiges of memory and insight, going back further and further into inarticulateness to try to make some sense . . . oh, it is too much, too much, Jennifer! Of course you warned me. I remember that distinctly and do not have to be reminded.

I do not have to be reminded of everything. I carry my culpability like a stain, my guilt like a stigmata; I can feel it rising off the skin in blotches sometime: *I feel responsible for every single injustice which has ever been done.* Psychosis, Jennifer, I am sinking fast, I really need some help. Jennifer I am sinking, Jennifer I am dying, Jennifer I am collapsing into the ooze of missed connections, failed networks; Jennifer I do not believe that I can stand this any longer, I need you, you have got to pull me out of the mire. I do not know how much more of this I can stand: the astronauts, turning inward on their stink and desperation in the last days of a homeward journey had nothing on me, dear; I can barely separate myself from the low twitches and mumblings of my mortality. You have got to help me, you are my wife or at least my ex-wife, you bear at least as much responsibility for my condition as I do because you were the one who, by leaving me, started the whole thing; everything would have been all right if you hadn't left me, it would not have come to this, you have got to do something Jennifer because if you do not the responsibility for what happens will be on your shoulders. Go to the authorities. Call the police. Tell them that something terrible is going to happen on *Revelations* Sunday night unless they do something, tell them that the proper authorities have got to take some meaningful action. You can do this, you are an Outsider. I charge you; you are responsible. If I mail this letter special delivery you will get it fast and there will be no excuses whatsoever if you fail to do what you must.

Jennifer I am collapsing, Jennifer I am dying, Jennifer I am folding in upon myself. Tell your husband that it was all a mistake and that you're taking a leave of absence. Tell your children that there are larger issues which they cannot possibly understand and that you are drawn to them. Tell the authorities that you are helping to implement the cause of justice should they complain. Come to me. You better come to me. This is absolutely your last chance.

It has been developing for a long time. Now it is almost here. I thought there was something going on; I thought the program was right, I thought the format was meaningful and Marvin Martin was on the side of destiny; I could not have done this otherwise. Now I see that I was wrong but I am doing everything I can to remedy the situation. You come to me and the two of us will go together to the chairman of the Federal Communications Commission and we will say, in tandem that is, "Sir, you must stop this. This is dangerously irresponsible and is giving people the wrong idea entirely of their lives and what they must do to alter them. It is cheating them of the very painful insights they must achieve to become human. It is cheating them of a sense of reverence for everything which bears the same name as they do. Also it is corrupt and probably manipulated in severe degree. As responsible adults in this country at this time we feel it our duty to say this. Stop the proceedings. Stop the show."

You can tell them that I was never basically the type of person who was right for this business, Jennifer.

You will tell them that, won't you, dear?

It just occurred to me that I do not recall your last address, since from the time you left I always had to reach you in care of a lawyer who has long since been disbarred and therefore there is no logical way to dispatch this letter. I will leave it in the rest of the notes I have compiled, however, trusting to luck and equity to somehow put me in touch with you and in the meantime, I will plow on as best I can.

I feel much better for having had the opportunity to write to you and hope that you are the same. You can reach me by return mail at the address above and I am looking forward to all of your thoughts on the matter as well as a plan of attack by which I can save *Revelations* and Monaghan from themselves and turn them back to the honorable course I envisioned so many years ago. With my best regards.

XL

Dear Mr. Hurwitz:

I know that this letter will never get through, they watch everything that I am doing but I just wanted you to know that I was serious, what I wanted to do was for the best, I had higher hopes and purposes and had no idea that it was this kind of situation or wouldn't have come this way. I have been through the most rigorous testing and training program known to man, I have dealt with the most monomaniacal and destructive bureaucracy in the history of the west but still I was completely unprepared for oh well I'm sure you know what I listen to me Mr. Hurwitz you have got to do something the police well the police would be interested but beyond that on the way to the moon I had a vision that space was inimical toward man utterly destructive but on the way back the vision turned and I saw that it was the other way around, we would kill everything we touched oh well you try to put it down the best you can and a certain resignation overtakes me; what did I expect anyway and where did I get the idea that the agency was more corrupt than anything else; the agency is American to the core, bound into the sense of America, a very native product indeed and it was to be expected that it all would have worked out that way strange how things have come to this point when once not so long ago they looked rational and reasonable I trusted you I thought that I could place myself in your hands and it is all your fault you better do something or in any event you better understand what is going on here I see that they are coming again so will close now I never wanted any part of this having something other in mind but after you are the 29th man on the moon you should have a good tragic sense and realize that from that bottoming-out point the rest is inevitable.

XLI

To Joan: You did pretty well under the circumstances. Thanks for the thoroughness of this final report. Why don't you take a leave of absence; work it out through channels, I will certainly approve two or three months with full pay and am duly grateful for your efforts. Everything worked out as expected and so little has been that way recently that I take the routine as a favor.

XLII

To Hurwitz: Your services are terminated as of this date. Two weeks pay are offered in lieu of notice.

Please leave these offices by eleven o'clock, turning in all keys. It is not necessary for you to arrange your desk other than for the removal of personal documents as you see fit. Your presence in these offices will not be tolerated after eleven this morning under any circumstances. Access to the studios is similarly barred and under no circumstances will you be permitted to attend the taping.

A letter of reference is enclosed as well as a statement of paid-in pension benefits from the accounting department.

XLIII

This is to certify that Michael Hurwitz has been in our employ as managing personnel specialist and that he can be recommended for any similar position that will make use of his abilities.

XLIV

PARTIAL TAPE OF REVELATIONS: #80. COPYRIGHT © 197– BY MARVMART PRODUCTIONS, INC., AND REPRODUCED THROUGH PERMISSION. THE RIGHT TO EXCERPT ANY OF THIS MATERIAL IS EXPRESSLY DENIED.

MARTIN: Tell me about your background, Monaghan. Sketched in briefly. Stop being so restless; everything here is under control.

MONAGHAN: Well, as I explained, I was affiliated with the space agency for seven years, participating in almost all of the duties of an astronaut, including a moon flight. After the moon flight I was put in a desk position—

MARTIN: Not by your own choice, however.

MONAGHAN: Not by my own choice, no. There were certain pressures—

MARTIN: You're really unbearably nervous, Monaghan. Can't you sit still?

MONAGHAN: I'm under a lot of pressure.

MARTIN: Only the pressure you're making on your own. No one's threatening you, no one is making you uncomfortable. I'm getting nervous, just looking at you.

MONAGHAN: I'm sorry. I'll try to stop.

MARTIN: It's hard to believe that an ex-astronaut would carry on this collection of nervous twitches, although astronauts aren't doing so well these days. Haven't you noticed this to be the case?

MONAGHAN: The program's been repudiated.

MARTIN: Why do you think that this is so?

MONAGHAN: Because it had no seeming effect upon the common lives of people. And it was used by the government as a means of misdirecting criticism, of putting people's attention somewhere else. Of course that didn't work. It never works.

MARTIN: That's interesting speculation, but you still haven't given us any significant personal details.

MONAGHAN: You haven't given me a chance.

MARTIN: You have all the time in the world. You reason tightly, Monaghan, but so far I see no sense of the personal.

MONAGHAN: How can you be personal? What kind of details can there be? The agency squeezes all the humanity out of everyone; turns them into machines. That's all I was, a machine; they fit you into a hole and you're supposed to stay in it. The personal is inextricably bound with the mechanical, after a while they mesh; they cannot be torn apart. I fought it, I've fought this ever since I got out and before that too but it isn't easy, it isn't—

MARTIN: You've given us reason to believe that the space flights were faked. That they were conducted hundreds of feet underground in the midwest in concealed television studios near the bomb-factories. That's a sensational charge. Can you defend it?

MONAGHAN: Of course. Of course they were—

MARTIN: Then you also offer statements that the flights were not faked, that only the public-relations aspects were and that several astronauts went insane during or shortly after the missions. How can you claim that there is any consistency between these stories?

MONAGHAN: Consistency. But they're *both* true. Both of them. Some of the flights, the *earlier* flights, were faked and then later on when they finally got the technology and started throwing people aboard it was with improper training and they couldn't take it. They had this time schedule, you see, and they had to meet it no matter what. They were slated to a target date and when it became obvious that they couldn't make it, they had to bail out the situation the other way. But then later. *Later*—

MARTIN: Which were you, one of the fakers, or one of those who went crazy?

MONAGHAN: I don't like you very much. I had respect for you once but now I'm losing it. You don't want to understand everything, you just want to torment me.

MARTIN: I've heard all that before. That material does not move me any more. I am an investigator and we are attempting to reach an understanding. This whole thing is depersonalized.

MONAGHAN: How can you say it's depersonalized? You *love* it. You *love* your work.

MARTIN: I despise my work and have for a long time. Scrub that one; knock that one off the tape. (Pause.) Did you actually land on the moon, Monaghan?

MONAGHAN: Of course I did. It's all been published.

MARTIN: I mean, in actuality. That wasn't studio fakery.

MONAGHAN: Oh no. No.

MARTIN: What was it like?

MONAGHAN: The moon?

MARTIN: What do you think?

MONAGHAN: It was all right. It was—vacant.

MARTIN: That's all.

MONAGHAN: That's about it.

MARTIN: You are the most unresponsive son of a bitch with whom I have ever dealt. I've only been on the air with you for ten minutes and already I despise you. Can you feel that?

MONAGHAN: I know that.

MARTIN: More and more I just despise the people with whom I deal; the vulnerable, empty little core of them, their stupidity, their greed. It is very hard to remain tolerant in the face of such unresisting gullibility and hopelessness. But you, Monaghan, are too much.

MONAGHAN: I wanted to tell my story.

MARTIN: It didn't used to be this way. There used to be some energy, enthusiasm. I would have the feeling that at last I was getting behind the mystery, the curtains were being torn apart, I was showing Americans the quality of their lives. There was a sense of mission to it; almost a mercy as well because we were coming close to the truth and without the truth there can be no forgiveness. Guilt can be canceled. I felt that there was hope, that there was meaning, that I was doing something useful. But it hasn't been that way for a long time now. Oh God, I'm tired, tired! Don't cut the tape this time; let it run. Get it all down. Stop protecting me, you sons of bitches; let them all see what's happened. More and more I feel like a man in darkness, a man sunken deep into the mud of his lost hopes, this man still strives for the light, makes gestures but it is all too late, he is going on old fuel and flames—

MONAGHAN: Maybe the world hasn't changed. Maybe you've changed.

MARTIN: You stay out of this. You don't exist any more. I thought that you would be different, that I could get something out of you. But you're all the same. All of you!

MONAGHAN: That's because you don't want to listen. That's because you haven't been dealing with people for years and years, Marvin Martin. When was the last time you faced someone? When was the last time you attempted to come to terms to connect. You're listening to the sound of your own voice, that's all: like an astronaut, the tinny, tiny sound of your own voice in the void reverberating back to you endlessly, the echoes collapsing in and out of your skull.

MARTIN: I really thought I was doing something worthwhile. When did it all begin to go wrong? If only I could pinpoint a time—

MONAGHAN: Until you began to look upon everyone with whom you dealt as the mirror of your own corruption, until you turned them into what you had become, that was what happened.

MARTIN: I don't know what you're doing. I don't even know who you are. What right do you have to do this to me on your program?

MONAGHAN: You know who I am.

MARTIN: Yes?

MONAGHAN: Face me. Face me. Now, can you see? Do you understand now? Do you see the man who is sitting across you. Face me for the first time, Martin; it's not too late, not too late if you can grasp—

MARTIN: Insane. This man is insane.

MONAGHAN: No I'm not; you tried to make me that way, you used all of your devices and enticements, your means and your manipulations to make me crazy but I'm not crazy, Marvin; I'm still sane and whole. I'm beyond you; don't you think that a man who went through what I did can take the likes of you? After a six-gravity pressure, what terrors can you hold? Do you know what happens to a man in six-g pressure? He blacks out and vomits; he collapses inside himself and when he regains consciousness, which is almost immediately thereafter, he feels that he has been wrenched inside and out but they don't want any part of that in the agency because you have to keep on sounding cheerful over the transmissions and above all you have to do the work; you have to keep the transmissions going, keep the pressure checks, do the manipulations and on-course changes, not because you have to because the whole thing is actually computer-controlled and there isn't a goddamned thing that you're needed to do but you've got to give the impression that you're busy working all the time, that you're completely in control, that everything is working out, that there's a rational, sane human being on top of the whole situation so you chatter away, chatter away and every minute of it you want to toss your guts out. Because you've got to be sane, competent and cheerful, most of all you have to be cheerful, that's the important thing. That's what killed the program, you know, the goddamned *cheerfulness* of it. If it hadn't always been so full of *chatter* and brightness it might have worked out.

MARTIN: Is that so?

MONAGHAN: You don't mean a thing to me, not a thing; your intimidation, your games, the noxious things you do to people before and during and after; you barely exist to me.

MARTIN: And you to me.

MONAGHAN: Face me! Face me! Do you know yet who I am? Can you see it in my eyes?

MARTIN: I see you. I see who you are. No! Don't stop! Let it go on. Let all of it go on, I want this down. Let it roll. Yes. Yes, I know who you are.

MONAGHAN: I've stalked you in a thousand nights, Martin; whirling in endless orbit I saw you too, saw your face, your eyes, waiting, dreaming of this engagement; I always knew that it would end this way. Didn't you?

MARTIN: Yes. Yes.

MONAGHAN: You must have dreamed it too; you must have dreamed me, the astronaut, the outsider, the man from the machine, you must have tossed with that vision as I tossed for yours and all the time although we did not know it we were being drawn, drawn inevitably to this constancy, a time when—

MARTIN: Don't stop it!

MONAGHAN: When we would meet at last and it would be seen fine and true and final, the two of us nested deep in machinery, this awful machinery to all sides of us, just like the inside of a capsule, terrible and odorous, small, dim and clanging; waiting for that moment when naked and face to face at last we could see—do you know what would happen?

131

MARTIN: I've waited. I've waited so long.

MONAGHAN: I know you have; I have too, the two of us thought that we were engaged in rational acts, going on our discrete ways but all the time it was only for this moment, twinning, the two of us linked together poles apart and now at last—

MARTIN: Oh God, I couldn't have waited any longer. It is time. It is time.

MONAGHAN: It's always been time, this has always been waiting; it was meant to be this way. Do you see it? Do you see now what I have in my hand?

MARTIN: Oh God, I should have known about the security that they would betray me—

MONAGHAN: Look at it, Martin; the deadly barrel, the blunt edges; this is what you've been waiting for, this has always been there at the end of dreams and now I raise it, raise the terrible snout and—

MARTIN: No! No! Not that. Stop the taping. For God's sake, stop it!

MONAGHAN: It can't be stopped, Marvin; they've been waiting for this too long. They've been holding against this moment; now at last it's come and they will not shut off the equipment. You have made assassins of all who surround you; have murdered everything surrounding their own murderous core and now it is too late, too unspeakably late, everyone will see—

MARTIN: All I wanted to do was to help people understand themselves! That's all! I never meant it to come to anything like this; you've got to believe it.

MONAGHAN: Too late, Marvin. It's too late.

MARTIN: I beg you—

MONAGHAN: It's too late for beggary; just as those who begged from you received no favors, similarly there are none here. Watch. Watch the handle, watch the butt, watch the trigger, watch the assassin advance.

MARTIN: For God's sake. No—

MONAGHAN: What did you expect, Marvin? Did you think that this would go on forever? (Tape ends.)

XLV

To Mills: I am enclosing herewith tapes of several broadcasts including the final one, several memoranda dealing with matters relevant to these tapes and a "journal" which was compiled by Michael Hurwitz and which touches on many of these matters (as well as extraneous ones) in great detail. I trust that you will find all of this satisfactory and by processing my forms DD-234H attached, agree that I have completed this assignment to the best of my ability and may now take that extended leave of absence which I was promised upon successful completion.

Hurwitz has not been seen since the time of the broadcast. His whereabouts are unknown; some of his associates seem to think that he may have committed suicide but I believe this is improbable. Knowing the man as I do and knowing his low cunning and sense of resource, I would suspect that he is still very much with us, hiding in mortal fear of discovery. Although for what reason I could not know.

There will be no trouble with the Communications Control Division; necessary parties as advised by you have been contacted and the matter has been resolved. *Revelations* is canceled as of the preceding broadcast and network will take responsibility for filling the time through the end of the season. The cover story on the natural death of Marvin Martin via heart attack went through well and I visualize no complications.

Monaghan, who accompanies these documents, has been debriefed in the customary manner and bears no memory whatsoever of these events. His disposition is entirely up to you and I make no recommendations. He has been a loyal employee and this should count on his behalf when disposition is made; on the other hand, it might be less embarrassing to have him permanently out of contact. You know how squeamish I am about these things. I have told him only a few necessary details sufficient to get him safely to you; he is under effective memory block. When the block is removed he will still retain the implantation, still think that he is an ex-astronaut and you take it from there. Technical details were never my strong point.

"I think we'll succeed," I remember you saying to me at our last interview before all this began, "but whether or not things will actually change in the removal of this program is something else; the ultimate joke may well be that things will turn out exactly the same and that *Revelations* was merely a symptom."

Well, now we shall see, shan't we, dear John? I think myself that this has been one hell of a circuitous way to do the deed but then, as you said, I never understood government too well, looking upon it always as an outsider.

I still have his bruises on my thighs, my buttocks, the part between my breasts. (This is not said to excite you.) The strange perversity of the man, the low cunning, the ferocity is something that I will not soon forget. Coming from the civil service as I do, I need a reminder every so often that people like this do exist. In the meantime I am claiming compensation.

And I want a long rest, John.

XLVI

Oh God I think I see this now; I really think I do but what's the point: what's the difference? It's all over and they even took my journal, stole it right under me the last time I was back and there's nowhere to put this down, nowhere that will tie it together; I see what has been going on, Hurwitz at last has delayed-knowledge but what to do, what to do? No more *Revelations*. No more *Revelations* for Hurwitz; he is gone and beyond that now, the poor stiff.

Only this, only this, the first time I saw Marvin Martin I was on a club car and the second time was after he hired me and that second time he leaned across the desk, all sincerity, all passion and said to me, "You understand, Hurwitz, that if we're any good at all, they'll destroy us. Not that that will stop me for a moment, nor that it will stop you. But you realize that if we ever begin to get into the center, they'll finish us off because we'll just be too dangerous. Now just file that away and do the best job you can, make us strong, make us dangerous. And meet them on their own ground."

And then things happened and I went to work and everything changed, even Marvin Martin, but I remember that now and I do not know, I simply do not know. Beast or saint he is finished now to say nothing of the grotesque Hurwitz and nothing more but small pieces of matter to be scraped up and filed where they never will be seen. Poor Marvin Martin! Poor Hurwitz! Poor Monaghan! Poor Jennifer!

Jennifer, I think of you now. It is Berne again, it is 1963; we sit in the sun. The wine is sauterne, we drink it, we touch hands, we look at one another foolishly; sounds come off the hills. From radios around us high peeping comes, the noise of information, bulletins, restlessness, riots, then we come to understand what has happened and now there is movement to the right and left of us, movement cutting through us who are its center and in the middle of it we sit stunned, our smiles turning to glass, the sauterne becoming acid in the cup, sit in the sun of Berne until it falls into the hills, the hills into the fields, the fields into the center of the earth and somewhere in the cone of this blackness we are sitting, we are sitting yet while the night falls down around us, choking like a collar and absolutely nothing to be done because the light of revelation is gone.

Garrison Avenue, 1971

AFTERWORD
FROM THE SECOND EDITION OF *REVELATIONS* (1976)

Barry N. Malzberg

Revelations was the first novel I wrote (exactly five years ago now) after moving to the house in northwest New Jersey which we still occupy. The opening chapters had been written in Manhattan late in 1970 and the contract secured before the move but, because I had a pretty fair idea of what the book was about and where I wanted to go with it, I deliberately held off on the writing until after the move. Fearful of a block in new premises, I wanted to have before me something on which I had a certainty. (Writers are not like that.) After having written approximately thirty-two novels in Manhattan, the last ten in a little, stuffy, odorous, clangorous maid's room with wall-to-wall radiators (described with vindictive accuracy in *Herovit's World*) I was afraid that I would be unable to function in a clean, well-lighted place surrounded by trees and the cries of birds attempting to clear northern New Jersey oil fumes from their little throats.

As it turned out I need not have worried. *Revelations* was written in three weeks and past a slight block which hung me on page 57 (in the original edition) for a while; it probably gave me as little trouble as any novel I wrote up until 1974. I went on to write more than three dozen novels amidst trees and oil-stricken birds. And when a certain narrowing of intensity, reluctance to continue my work, and loss of facility occurred about a year ago, it had nothing to do with the environment in which I was writing. So in one sense *Revelations* is close to my heart; whatever its defects it proved to me, when I was still (despite my prolificacy and growing reputation in the field of science fiction), not quite sure of what I was doing that I was able to write from a level where I was precise indeed.

I am fond of this novel. I enjoyed writing it—or parts of it (or at least I did not write it as I have written most of my books of the last five years in terrible pain)—and reread it on publication and before this resale with as much pleasure as I can bring to my own work. It freed me from the fear of a block at what might have been a bad time (men may feel this way about otherwise ordinary women who they have met and been loved by at crucial moments of their lives) and it also strikes me, *pace* Pronzini, as being one of my five—or at the worst ten—most successful novels. It is also one of the few novels I have written about which I have something to say beyond the text and it is in that spirit that I would like to turn to the book itself now, moving from circumstance to interior instead of interior to circumstance which is my more usual writing method—one particularly visible in *Revelations* itself.

Revelations was written just about midway between *The Falling Astronauts* (February, 1971) and *Beyond Apollo* (July and August 1971) and shares with them not only certain obsessions and characters representative of that time—mad astronauts; sexual dysfunction as representing the necessary loss of energy of the machine age; the single human voice crying in madness or in truth out through the network of the machines as a last hopeless expression of the idiosyncratic heart before the darkness of the great engines—but a certain similarity in development as well. In all three novels the protagonist has been emotionally devastated by the failure of a space voyage; in all three he is trying to understand the failure in a way that will explain him to himself. The difference among the three novels is at least as crucial however: in *Falling Astronauts* the protagonist breaks down only at the end of the book; in *Beyond Apollo* he is crazy from the opening lines. *Revelations*, that transitional novel, is equivocal. Hurwitz is mad but then again he is not; he is quit beyond the line but he is the only character on the *Revelations* television program who is trying to establish emotional links to what is going on, the only one who has some sense of responsibility left. He is on the way toward coming apart but he is not precisely there.

At one time I thought that *Falling Astronauts* was a first draft of *Beyond Apollo*, that the latter novel was the former, darker and more compressed, with almost all of the *events* taken out. Pure state of mind, in fact. When I read *Revelations* however I understood that it was not quite as simple as that. This novel is a key step on the way from the rather ambitious but narratively clumsy and lumpish *Falling Astronauts* to the fugal interstices of *Beyond Apollo* which is as technically seamless as *Falling Astronauts* is technically flawed. In *Revelations* I was beginning to transmute the material and come to grips with it by squeezing the pain out, putting the narrative density in, but I was not quite there yet. Oddly, this may be to the effect that *Revelations* is the best of the three novels. *Beyond Apollo*, which had an audience and is certainly the most commercially successful of my science fiction novels, is perhaps too private, too off-putting and cold whereas *Falling Astronauts* even in its best scenes lives for me as little more than a competent attempt at a competent commercial novel. It is not fully controlled. *Revelations* may get the best of the two books—the event of *Astronauts*, the rhetoric and dreadful pain of *Apollo*—and in fact may be a terminal treatment of the theme. Perhaps it and not *Apollo* tied off the paranoid astronaut, the terrible strictures of NASA, which so obsessed me from the years 1969 to 1971. (It is true that after *Beyond Apollo* I quit. Barring one short story, "Notes Leading Down to the Disaster" in April 1972, I never touched the theme again. I work my obsessions over endlessly but only to a point and when I am done with them at last they are done. I have not written about horse racing for that matter since the summer of 1970 or institutionalized sex since the beginning of 1974. So there is hope for some new material by the eighties, my friends.)

At the time that I first tied into this theme, just about the time of the Borman moon-circling and bible-thumping mission of Christmas 1968, I was the only science fiction writer there. Later on there were many of us (and as I write this I read that Brian Stableford, a good young British SF writer, has just published a novel about a lunatic selected to head a mission to Mars) but modesty does not forbid me from saying that I was the first and that I found, at the dying end of the 1960s and of the space program, one of the last few new directions which the decadent field of science fiction has been able to produce.

That direction, to be explicit about this, was the theme of space exploration by bureaucracy being dehumanizing *not* because space was that way—because we have never understood what we are; because only in space might we find new parameters of the definition of being human—but because bureaucracy was. The attempt by NASA and the Johnson and Nixon administrations to make space exploration merely an extension of American industry on the one hand and the government civil service on the other, struck me as absolutely despicable and also hopeless.

It was despicable because it was despicable—we can barely claim the right to our own hearts; we cannot claim cosmos—but more to the point it was hopeless because 95 per cent of Americans (at least) loathe, fear and disbelieve their government. If space was to be perceived as a product of a government agency, then it was only a matter of time (and very little time as it turned out) before the population turned away from the space program and the government, finding it no longer useful as a device of entertainment or repression, and would similarly abandon it. I saw all of this coming as early as July 21, 1969 when Edward Kennedy's Chappaquidick was already beginning to crowd the front page of the *New York Times* for space as against the Moon landing and I was positive when Apollo 13 was almost lost in transit that I had been right . . . because the reaction of most people I knew to Apollo 13 was that the entire disaster had been rigged by NASA and by Nixon to reestablish public interest in the program.

By 1971, Gardner Dozois reported to me, the news of yet another moon landing announced at a science fiction convention, of all places, attracted no interest whatsoever. In the entertainment culture very little holds past twenty-six or at the most thirty-nine weeks. By 1971 there were new concerns in the government—like putting every American slightly to the left of Mike Mansfield in jail within a few years—and by 1973, of course, several very funny things had happened to all of us on the way to the concentration camps.

I saw it all coming . . . the collapse of the space program, that is to say, the collapse of NASA and the Cape and the Houston program. Even as I saw it I cried out in rage because it was never space exploration against which I had taken a position, but merely its capture, in contemporary America, by a repressive government operating through an enormous bureaucracy that was dead of feeling, careless of hope. We deserved better than all of this I thought; we did indeed deserve—would find it necessary—to continue outward and inward toward the other planets. But the government did not care, could not understand. By the middle of the seventies they had taken not only large pieces of our past from us, but almost all of our future.

How right I was in seeing that the structure of the program and its administration would drive many astronauts crazy we have only been intimating in recent years . . . because I *was* right about that. I knew from the beginning that my insights were correct, I knew that the men going into those capsules— ostensibly as operators, actually as cargo—would be forced to come to terms with the devastating fact *that they could serve only by being machinery* and that many of them, sensi- tive and reflective as all of us in our better moments would wish them to be, could not easily deal with this fact. Only years later did we learn of the divorces, the breakdowns, the lurches into mysticism, the scattered children, the pain that the bureaucracy had inflicted upon some of these astronauts but by then of course *Revelations* and *Falling Astronauts* and *Beyond Apollo* were out of print or nearly so, and even if they had not been it hardly would have mattered.

There is no percentage in this culture in trying to tell the truth for any reason although at the time I was writing these books there was a certain amount of diversity permitted in the culture and I was making a fair living on advances. It all seems a long way in the past now. So does *Revelations*. For a novel of the future (near-future, granted), it seems, like many science fiction novels, to be curiously dated. Science fiction of course was almost never meant to be about the future, it was merely another category of escape literature constructing templates of the present for the momentary diversion of readers . . . but certain novels like *More Than Human* and *The Demolished Man* seem timeless whereas others like *A Canticle for Leibowitz* or *Fahrenheit 451* or *Revelations* seem to be very much of a time, already framed in retrospection when come back to years later. How nearly quaint all of these astronauts, moon shots, endorsements, and anguish seem today! I think that I made only one error in the three astronaut books that may turn out to be serious: I knew that it was all going down the tube but somehow back then I thought that its participants and certain witnesses might care a little more. They do not, of course. If I were to rewrite *Revelations* today—I do not see how I could do it—it would be an emotionless book written with far more humor and Monaghan would have felt almost no pain at all. Like his fucking, his dialogues with Martin Miller would have all been beside the point. For fun or for shame, in short, but not for pain.

But I am not rewriting the novel today; it is five years later and I cannot (and should not) get back to the writer I was any more than we can get back to the dimly remembered world of the late sixties of which 1971 was simply a pale, weak, and final extension. It had been my intent at the time I placed the novel with Avon to go through it, do some cutting here, a little expanding there—maybe try to take a little of the edge from that hysteria. But on due consideration I am not. Leave it. Let it stand. A novel (or at least a seriously intended novel) may be an attempt at art but it is also a work of documentary, witness, testimony, and becomes its own small piece of sacred ground. *Revelations* shows where my heart and certain fragments of the culture were in April of 1971. Let it be. Let it make the record. Let us not cheapen the concept of rediscovery as the whores of the Bicentennial Commission have cheapened it by feeling that we must clean up the past to make it work. The founding fathers, some of them, were racists with bad teeth. Malzberg in 1971, as now, had his flaws as a writer. Leave them be. To know what we have been is to move at least a little toward knowing what we are . . . and to know what we are is the first step toward becoming human. Which I still take, which I still aver, to be a value.

One final anecdote, *orbiter dicta* but possibly as relevant as anything above. I mentioned hitting a block on page 57 that lasted three hours or so (well, I was younger then, just a big, heavy, lovable kid with a triple chin; I didn't know what the hell I was doing then or for many years thereafter; the latest block from which I am just beginning to stagger has lasted thirteen months) but bothered me and in the middle of it Robert Silverberg called and returned a favor. In the summer of 1970 Silverberg had told me over the phone that he had hit a bad point in *Tower of Glass* somewhere around page 120, didn't know where to go. "Literary it up Bob," I said and he said, "My God, that's it," and hung up quickly. He told me years later that he had directly gone to do ten pages of stream-of-consciousness which had gotten him past a kink in the plot and had sent him rolling on cheerily toward the not-so-cheering ending (his "great gong that sounds in the heavens" in the last paragraph of that novel strikes me as the most moving literary image of our time). Now, I asked him, what the hell to do with this narrator/protagonist who had a brilliant rhetoric but an acute case of spiritual constipation which was already on page 66 of copy wearying me. "How about a perfect Arcadian vision?" Silverberg said, "have a whole chapter of him imagining a better, an ideal life."

So I said thank you and hung up quickly and came back to this very office and wrote Hurwitz-as-prep-school-teacher in about fifteen minutes, pulling the novel along, getting my narrator off the pot and building in a new level of insight almost effortlessly. Pages 58-62 I owe to Robert Silverberg as well as many other things: I take yet another opportunity to say that I consider him (no longer within easy phone reach, alas) the best living writer in the language.

It is April of another year although now and then I think that it must be the same bird gasping in the tree outside; certainly it must be the same squirrel gnawing away in the gutter and leader overhead. It is the same office and desk although another typewriter and in the most crucial sense another person is sitting here. Here, down here in the dream quarter while the night falls down around us, choking like a collar and absolutely nothing to be done because the light of revelation is gone.

AFTERWORD TO AN AFTERWORD
CULTURAL APPROPRIATION AND ITS DISCONTENTS (2019)

Barry N. Malzberg

The fate of a novel like *Revelations* when published as a paperback original is so common (and therefore so predictable) that any complaint would be *obiter dicta*; I knew where I was going and what I was getting and the advance on this novel covered with something to spare the closing costs on the house to which I had moved a few weeks before this was written. If you expect nothing you are more likely to get that heart's desire and the surreal cover of the Warner Paperback Library edition indicated, at least, that the artist more or less understood the point I was trying to make. Later on it became apparent that there were others.

Five years later, upon the release of the film *Network* in 1976, it was immediately apparent to me (and to a spare and scattered population at least as helpless) that although *Revelations*, a paperback original from a second-line publisher, had sunk into the desert of anonymity, it had had at least one extraordinarily attentive reader. Paddy Chayefsky understood it just fine. *Network* was released a little more than half a decade after the novel's publication and its anticipatory chronicle of "reality" television and one power-mad host limned with fair precision a form of televised entertainment which had barely existed. The furious amalgamation of the political and the personal, the maudlin and the desperate, the audience and its desire was pretty well limned in this novel and the narrative came out in a span of two to three weeks, written in a furious clarity which seems about as crazy as it was credible. As the 1976 afterword (written for the Avon Books Science Fiction Rediscovery program) stated, the novel was composed in a cocoon of anger and fear, and if I did not know exactly what I was doing (a relatively common situation), I certainly knew what the perceptions in which *Revelations* wallowed were doing to me. They scared me like hell.

I guess that they scared Chayefsky too because he was one of the closest observers of television in his time and indeed had used it early on as the medium for one-hour television plays which made his career. One of them, *Marty*, doubled in length as a movie, won an Academy Award, and as television drama gave way to sitcoms and movies of the week, he was able to make the transfer to Hollywood seem inevitable. *Network* was both a recherche to times lost and a predictive work; the mad-as-hell anchor and the broadcast assassination for remuneration by a recruited team of revolutionary warriors were Chayefsky's exploration of what he took to be the medium's inevitable destination. Television "news" would no longer report the event but would *become* the event. That was the stated purpose of Chayefsky's documentary program and also of my own *Revelations*. Ultimately the reportage and the event would fuse, would become one another, would in fact become indistinguishable.

Into this landscape I recruited a crazed astronaut (or pseudo-astronaut) from two earlier novels, *The Falling Astronauts* and *Beyond Apollo*, on a campaign to prove that the Apollo program and its conquest of space was a hoax. I intended to amalgamate the madness and paranoia of my protagonist, assistant to Marvin Martin the television host, for profit motif with the lunatic sprawl of *Falling* and *Apollo*. It was a capsulization of those earlier works, the conclusion or at least apotheosis of what I conceived as an approximation of a trilogy, and it made (Salinger's phrase) a kind of prose home movie, an earthers' version of the two earlier and more distant novels. If I could bring it off—this compound of craziness—by proving that mad astronauts and mad documentation were essentially indistinguishable, well then I would have a trilogy which would explain as no one had yet explained, not even the brilliant Englishman J.G. Ballard, why the space program in its institutionalization, denial and evasion of the central argument was doomed. Apollo 11 was not a launch but a curtain call; Apollo 13 (in its futile dramatics or dramatic futility) was a coda, and after the reassurance of the last missions, the program was finished. I felt that there would never be another Moon landing, let alone colonization, let alone a brave conquest of Mars within the lifetime of anyone then present on the planet. I think that this is in the latter stage of proving out, as they would have said in Houston.

That left me with a novel which had essentially been plundered for useful profit, discarded for the rest, and had a very small readership over the half-century which regarded *Revelations* as visionary without in any way being able to do anything about it. A "rediscovery" edition less than five years after the original publication was merely a validation of doom and did not leave me feeling affirmative. "If I am being 'rediscovered' at the age of 37, if I already am eligible that soon for recusal from the forgotten . . ." Well, this bleak news was in effect its own message.

Apollo was intended as a diversion for the public from the increasingly murderous course in Vietnam; Apollo was also, as John W. Campbell told me happily, "about the only government activity in which the public could see directly their money put to some use and it was terrifically entertaining." And when Vietnam (and for that matter the most visible element of Government) collapsed in the mid-seventies, there was no apparent rationale for Apollo. The space shuttles were a kind of holding action, but Challenger in 1986 took care of the ad astra component, and the issue of space exploration, let alone colonization, has become little more than a talking point for campaigns. "Are you against it or *strongly* against it?" is close to the central question of the day.

In sum, here is my novel embarked upon its third and probably final go-round. Like all of science fiction, it was written as a commentary of the present, dressed in the drag of the future. Chayefsky's film certainly met that construct, the novel less so because it had both larger and smaller issues as the central concern. This is the most ambitious of the astronaut trilogy, goes the furthest afield, struggles with its movement over and again to change the subject. It is fair testimony. Ballard—who I never met—would agree, I hope. I don't know what Chayefsky's opinion might have been, but he was willing, I am sure, to take what honor and circumstance gave him. He died almost 40 years ago at 58; I am writing this meditation at an age he never, by 22 years, got to be. He won the Oscar; I was the subject of a special issue of *DeLap's Science Fiction Review* in the year of the film's release. Be the pari-mutuel crowd and you pick the winner. Some of those games go a long way back, D. Harlan . . .

REVELATIONS

ABOUT THE AUTHOR

BARRY N. MALZBERG is an American writer, editor, and agent. His prolific career has spanned numerous genres, most notably crime and science fiction. Malzberg was particularly active in the SF scene of the early seventies, although he became disillusioned with the market forces defining the field and has rarely published SF works since. His most recent activity in the field has been in the form of advice columns for writers in the quarterly magazine of the Science Fiction and Fantasy Writers of America. Malzberg won the first John W. Campbell Memorial Award for *Beyond Apollo* in 1973. Over the years, his writing has been shortlisted for the Hugo, Nebula, and Philip K. Dick Awards, among others.

OTHER AOP TITLES

AN EARNEST BLACKNESS
Eugen Bacon

A SHORT, SHARP SHOCK
Kim Stanley Robinson

CITY PRIMEVAL
Robert Carrithers & Louis Armand

GALAXIES
Barry N. Malzberg

ENTROPOLOGY
Louis Armand

SPECTRE
Laurence A. Rickels

JACKANAPE & THE FINGERMEN
D. Harlan Wilson

NOSTALGIA
Hope Jennings

SHRAPNEL: CONTEMPLATIONS
Lance Olsen

SOFT INVASIONS
James Reich

TAO TE JINX: APHORISMS & QUOTATIONS
Steve Aylett

THE BLOT
Jonathan Lethem & Laurence A. Rickels

THE WAKE & THE MANUSCRIPT
Ansgar Allen

www.ingramcontent.com/pod-product-compliance
Lightning Source LLC
Chambersburg PA
CBHW020652260626
47157CB00008B/3000